Delicate

A WICKED HEARTS STORY

SARA CATE

Delicate

Editor: Rumi Khan

www.saracatebooks.com

Give feedback on the book at:
admin@saracatebooks.com

Printed in the U.S.A

Chapter One

SIERRA

The buzzing sound is relentless. It's like knives drilling into my head. How anyone could work here all day, I don't know. It seems impossible.

"So you think I should do the dolphin or the dragonfly?" Natalie says next to me, flipping through her phone. She has a Pinterest board pulled up with hundreds of girly tattoo images on the screen.

"I don't know," I answer. "Which one has more meaning to you?"

"Eh. I don't really care about meaning. I just want something pretty back there, you know?" She winks as she points to her left shoulder blade.

I laugh, although it's a little forced. She's the kind of girl with a perfect body—round hips, thin hourglass waist, and big, full breasts that make the most boring T-shirt look smoking hot. I'm a little jealous.

"Natalie," a man's voice calls in a flat tone from the front desk. I recognize the big, burly man with the salt and pepper beard, dashing green eyes, and broad, hard shoulders.

Natalie jumps up from her seat to greet him—with her boobs, of course. He doesn't even notice. I have no doubt that Natalie is not above sleeping with him just because he's a decade or more older.

"Logan is gonna be right out to do your ink. Did you decide on anything?"

"Oh, you're not doing it?" she asks, leaning over the glass. I roll my eyes at her display. Natalie and I have known each other for years, but we only hang out when our parents come up to Wickett Beach on holidays—or Wicked Beach, as it's been unofficially renamed. I like Natalie, but she and I are two totally different people. She flaunts everything all the time and doesn't even care that guys only want her for one thing.

Which is fine. But it just seems to take all of the fun out of it for me. It might sound cliché, but when I find the right guy, I want it to be special—not just a quick romp for fun.

She's still trying to get the older guy to react to her tit

display, but he doesn't seem impressed. I bet he sees girls like her all the time, especially this week.

Spring break on Wicked is typically crazy, full to the brim with young, rich trust fund babies in the prime of their first week of freedom. Bars and clubs are more relaxed on their carding policy. Cops let the rules go because more people are spending money, and it's known for being a playground for the rich kids. Not quite as sleazy as Cancún, but just as wild.

While we wait, I glance around the shop. It's decorated like a mechanic's garage with big red toolboxes and short black stools on wheels, which is clever and somehow sexy. The front desk is a glass case full of photos and piercing jewelry. It's actually a pretty tasteful place and not what I expected. I've only ever seen it from the outside, and I was picturing something seedier. My parents would freak if they knew I was in here, but just like every spring break on Wicked, they disappear and leave me alone for the entire week.

I'm an adult now, so it's not like I need a chaperone anymore. But if they knew where I was, I bet they would disagree. I smile to myself thinking about their reaction.

The thought of shocking them makes me strangely happy.

"Natalie?" Another man appears from behind the wall that divides the front waiting area and the back where the tattoos are taking place. I glance up when I hear his voice, smooth and deep like chocolate, and my jaw nearly hits the floor. I can't take my eyes off of him. He's covered from his hands to his neck in tattoos, but they're not all black like the older guy's. They're beautiful, vibrant, and full of color like a mural on his skin. In fact, I don't think there is any black in them at all—like a watercolor.

But it's not his tattoos that keep my attention. It's his familiarity.

I know him.

Every summer I come to the island, I seek him out, in the least creepy way possible, of course. Once or twice, I would gawk at him through the window as I passed on the boardwalk. More than once, I watched him eating at the diner down the street.

Why I've been so drawn to him, and act like a stalker suitable for a true crime documentary, I don't know.

It's not just his looks, and I mean, he is gorgeous, with his rich brown hair that always falls in perfect waves over his forehead and his sharp cheekbones. Maybe that's what caught my eye the first time I saw him back when I was just fourteen, but the fascination became something more than that.

I could see the trouble in his eyes, like he held secrets I wanted to know and wisdom I could never understand. He can't be more than twenty-five, but I can just tell his twenty-five years have seen a lot more than my nineteen.

"That's me!" Natalie squeals, and as soon as her eyes land on him, she seems to forget the guy behind the counter.

But he's not looking at her. He's looking at me.

I'm still sitting on the folded black chairs as we stare at each other, and I feel a settling weight of remorse land in my gut. Something about him has changed since last year. It's not just the new tattoos or the way his shoulders don't seem to fill out the T-shirt in the same way they did before. There's a little less life behind his eyes.

I stand and walk toward Natalie, trying to pull myself from the trance I fell into the second his crystal blues fell on me. "It's her," I say as I point to my friend.

"You don't want a tattoo?" he replies with a crooked smile. It's contagious because I feel my own smile grow across my face. Without knowing why, I put my hand against my cheeks to hide the grin. The world's worst flirter, right here.

"N-no," I stutter.

He shows his pearly white teeth, and I swear my knees buckle.

Natalie cackles next to me. "Her? Get a tattoo? Yeah, right." I realize she's teasing me, so I lose my smile and glare at her. I get that I look a little innocent, but I'm no saint.

"Well, maybe one day," he says, and I'm under the spotlight of his stare again.

"I think I want a dolphin on my shoulder here," Natalie says, pointing to her back. "To remind me of my time here. It's special to me," she says, looking at him through heavy lids.

He nods at her and takes a deep breath, an expression I can tell means he's mentally preparing himself to deal with yet another bubbly young girl and her dolphin tattoo.

I smile to myself as I follow them back to his station.

LOGAN

God, I fucking hate spring break. It's nothing but drunk, rich fucks and dolphin tattoos.

But the business is good, so I guess I shouldn't complain. Murph loves the girls this time of year, but I could live without them. They come to Wickett (I refuse to call it Wicked) once a year to get their kicks with the dirty locals and take off back to their lives of big houses and upstanding boyfriends. We are a proverbial bucket list for these girls.

I lost a bet to Murph, hence why I'm stuck with the dolphin, and he gets to take the next walk-in. The shop was slow for a minute, and I bet him the next customer to walk in would be a frat guy on a drunk dare. It's past 8:00 p.m. on the first night of spring break. Getting a stupid tattoo is like a rite of passage. But when we heard the door bells ring, we both peaked our heads around to see two girls walk in. One looking like she was ready to fuck the coat stand if someone didn't step up. And the other...was her.

I never thought I'd live to see the day she'd actually walk into the shop. She spent the last five years watching from afar, which made sense. A girl like her doesn't belong here. With her white Chucks and a pink skirt that hangs from her barely-there hips, this girl couldn't look more out of place if she tried.

"Ha ha," Murph teases. "You're up."

"Okay, go get them signed in. Let me grab a smoke, and I'll be right up."

"Fine," he bellows. Then his hand lands firmly on my shoulder. "A smoke." His eyes narrow, and I nod back.

Fuck, I know he's just worried about me, but I hate being treated like I need to be babysat. Whatever I want to do behind the shop is my fucking business.

And if I want to chase the sweet, sweet ecstasy of the powered bliss in my pocket, that's my choice.

Although I am working, and it's his business, so maybe I will just wait until after my shift to do anything other than smoke. The little plastic bag feels like it's burning a hole through my pants and into my skin. Damn, I wish it would.

He says I have no self-control, but look at me. Waiting until after my shift to get high.

The girl up front is being obnoxious. I can hear her through the back door. When I come back in, I do the usual routine: wash my hands, prep my supplies, and sanitize the seat and everything in my station. I have to appreciate how clean and righteous Murph runs things here. I wouldn't work anywhere else.

Rounding the corner to the front of the shop, I stop in my tracks when I see the girl again. But this time, my eyes aren't on her squeaky-clean sneakers or pastel pink skirt. I'm drawn to her eyes, nearly as blue as mine. Why haven't I ever really looked into those big doe eyes before?

Every line of her face is delicate.

I have to snap out of it before I make a fool of myself staring at this beautiful mystery girl.

After I call the client, Natalie, she starts babbling on about a dolphin, and it takes every ounce of resolve in my body to not groan.

I don't know why I tease the blonde about getting a tattoo. I think I want to see her smile, and it's perfect. This girl is not my type, but I still want to look at her, hear her voice, swim in those perfect blue eyes.

When we reach my station, Natalie straddles the chair and immediately pulls down her shirt where she wants the dolphin. We make small talk while I clean the area and draw the design onto her skin. She chatters about coming to Wickett every spring and how she loves getting down with the locals. I fake my laughter through her story, and then my eyes slide up toward the quiet girl sitting in a chair in the corner.

"What about you?" I ask.

She lifts her eyes expectantly.

"Do you love to get down with the locals?" I tease her. Natalie giggles until I remind her to hold still.

"She's not really the get-down type," Natalie whispers.

"That's okay."

"I love coming here. Not to get down with the locals," she answers, mimicking our tone, "but just because people are nicer, and I can breathe better here."

Glancing up again, I smile because I know exactly what she means. Wickett has always been like that for me. Quiet. Comfortable. Every other week of the year.

"Boring," Natalie mumbles as I hold a mirror up to show her the sketch on her back. "Yes, I love it," she says. I ready the ink and listen to the girls talk about their plans after the tattoo. They're going down to the bonfire which is a spring break ritual. They do it every year, and it's always packed down there with tons of rich college kids, a real kickoff to the week.

Not gonna lie, I don't like the idea of this girl going down to the bonfire. It's notorious for heavy drinking and rowdiness. Every year some douchebags end up going a little far, and it becomes town gossip quick. The cops don't do much with the pressures from the investors. I get the inside scoop from my brother's best friend on the force. He hates this week even more than I do.

They let the kids have their fun but try to keep it under control. And they usually do.

Until I show up with my pocket full of party favors.

When I press my foot on the pedal, Natalie jumps

from the loud buzz of the gun. I can already tell this is going to suck. She will cry and squirm, and it will turn out like shit. And I fucking hate when it's not perfect.

"Is this going to hurt?" she whines.

"No, it tickles," I answer dryly.

Two seconds into the tattoo, she's crying. I don't even get a full outline before she turns stark white and her skin goes cold.

"I'm going to throw up," she cries.

I lift my foot from the pedal and grab her a bottle of water. Setting the tattoo gun on the tray, I help her up from her seat. "You need fresh air."

"We can help you to the door. Can you walk?" the girl asks.

"I think so," Natalie mumbles.

God, I fucking hate fainters. Every once in a while, I get the pukers and the fainters. I pull off my gloves and help Natalie to the back door—never out the front. It's bad for business. She sits on one of the chairs we have back there for this exact reason.

"Put your head between your legs, honey. Deep breath in and deep breath out."

"It smells back here," she whines.

"Yeah, it's an alleyway behind a tattoo shop, and we're fresh out of candles," I reply dryly. I shouldn't be such a jerk, but I'm irritable, and the bag in my pocket isn't getting any lighter.

The blonde girl laughs to herself as she pats Natalie's back. It's a nice laugh, and it pulls me from my sour mood. I lean back against the cool bricks and reach for my cigarettes, but when her eyes follow my hands, I stop. It's weird for me, but I don't want to smoke in front of her. I smoke in front of everyone, and I normally don't care who knows it.

Her eyes meet mine, and I feel myself get lost again in her soft features. "Are you sure you don't want a tattoo?" I ask, wanting to fill the silence with her voice.

"I'm sure. There's nothing I want on my skin forever. Nothing that means that much to me," she says as she shrugs her tiny shoulders.

"That can't be true. There must be something you love."

The corners of her mouth lift into a tricky smile.

"Let me guess," I say, feeling more flirtatious than normal. "You like music. You play the piano..."

She shakes her head.

"Okay...tennis?"

Her face twists into a scowl, like I've offended her.

"Cheerleading?"

"You're terrible at this," she teases me.

This small-talk-banter between us is natural but also strange. Like we're both ignoring the fact that we've seen each other from afar for years, but this is the first actual encounter between us.

"Sorry," I laugh. Looking at her for another long moment, I take another guess. "I bet you love to read."

"There you go. I do love to read."

"Ah-ha. I knew I'd get it."

"You're a little harder to guess," she says, squinting her eyes at me.

"Not really," I say, wanting a cigarette again.

She's about to say something else when Natalie sits up. Her face has a little more color than before. "I think I can do it this time. I promise."

"Let's try this again." I lead the two of them back into the shop, but I don't miss how Blondie has a shy smile on her face as she passes me through the doorway.

Chapter Two

LOGAN

The shop quiets down a little after midnight. Murph is still working on an arm piece, but there hasn't been any new walk-ins since the girls. Natalie actually sat through the rest of her dolphin tatt, but not without crying and whining the whole time.

My phone buzzes in my pocket as I sweep the floor around my station. I already know who it is.

Step outside. Let's chat.

My shift is technically over, so I sneak out the back door without Murph even noticing. Hale is already out there, leaning against the wall across the alley. His shaggy blond hair is hanging over his eyes as he stares down at his phone.

Hale doesn't look like your usual drug dealer. Maybe that's how he's gotten away with it for so long. He's a trust fund brat like the rest of them, but instead of pursuing stocks and bonds or whatever it is that these kids do for money, he found something much more lucrative.

"Spring break, bitches," he jokes in a high-pitched voice. "There's a crowd at the bonfire now. I figured you might want to go check it out."

I pull out a cigarette and light it. The small bag in my pocket is still burning itself into my skin, but I don't want to touch it. It's not something I'm comfortable doing in front of Hale. Considering I still owe him over four hundred, it feels like a punch in the face to smoke my debt right in front of him, so I settle for a cigarette.

This is how he corners me into selling for him, to pay off my debt. Meanwhile, he keeps his image clean, and in a small community like Wickett, the plan is pretty flawless.

Well, not for me. I tend to rack up debt faster than I can pay it, and he knows that. Hence why he sticks with me. That and the fact that I have a way with these kids, especially the girls.

No, I'm not proud of myself, but these punks show up once a year, trash our beautiful beach, use and abuse us, then leave. What the fuck do I care if they get a little kick while they're here? At least they can afford to get hooked. Unlike the rest of us.

"I'll have to go down there and say hello," I say with the cigarette hanging from my lips. I can barely smoke it. I'm just in a funk tonight. I agree to go to the beach, but my heart isn't in it. All I can think about is that Sandra Dee blonde with her perfect white shoes and soul-piercing blues, and I just don't give a shit about smoking or bonfire bitches. I suddenly wish I was the kind of guy who could cozy up to her on a night like tonight. And I've never thought like that before.

"They're just getting started, so you might want to hustle. And you know...hustle." He laughs at his own lame joke, and I'm reminded that this kid is still clean as fuck.

"Yeah, let me just clean up around here, and I'll head down there." I reach my hand out toward him, keeping an eye on the alley way to make sure there isn't anyone watching or walking by. He hands me a plastic bag full of smaller bags. It isn't much, but with what they will pay, it doesn't need to be much. I shove it into my pocket and clap his hand before turning to walk back into the shop.

"I'll catch up with you tomorrow," he calls to me as he walks away. I don't think he looked up from his phone once during our entire conversation. But I don't really care. I'd rather not have a relationship with him. Or anyone, for that matter.

SIERRA

There's a crowd around the fire, and they're all getting so drunk it will be a miracle if they make it through this night without anyone falling in. I'm sitting on the wooden log that acts as a bench. Natalie is showing off her tattoo to anyone that will listen. She's already pulled off the plastic even though Logan told her to keep it on for eight hours.

"The boys will be here soon," she says as she sits next to me. She hands me another beer, but I'm not even half done with the one I'm holding. I don't bother to tell her that there are already a hundred boys at this bonfire, but apparently she's waiting for two specific boys. One of them I know she hooked up with last year and apparently he was into it, because he wants to hook up again.

And she said he's bringing a friend for me. Or I guess it sounded more like she needed me to come with her because he said that she needed a friend for his friend. Whichever way it went down, I'm not feeling really into it. It's past midnight, and I don't know where two guys could be up until midnight that doesn't sound shady and two-timing, but I don't think she really cares. That's what spring break on Wicked is all about. Bang as much as possible, no repercussions. No hang-ups. Start on Sunday. End on Sunday.

I haven't told Natalie that I have not and will not be

hooking up with anyone at any point this week. She may be okay with losing her virginity to a drunk frat boy under the docks or in the back of a dirty truck, but I am not.

"Hey, baby!" a voice bellows from behind as he practically lands on my lap. This must be Natalie's friend. He has his arm around me as she jumps into his, and I can't get him to let me go as he starts kissing her. When he pulls away, he looks at me, and all I can smell is the beer on his breath.

"Oh my God, you whores. Who is this?" he says as he leans in toward me. I lean away, trying to fake a laugh, as Natalie tries to pull him off of me.

"That's Sierra. Where is your friend?" she asks.

"Oh! Tyler!" he screams across the crowd of people around us.

God, I just want to go home. This is the definition of pure hell.

"Grant, get up. I want to show you my new tattoo," Natalie whines at the drunk boy still hanging on me.

He stares into my eyes as if he thinks we're actually making some deep connection. It's disconcerting, but I finally stand, just to get him to back off a little bit.

Tyler—I'm assuming—comes up behind Natalie and high fives Grant. "Hey, man, this party is lit."

"Yeah, man. This is Sierra," he says, putting his arm back around me, and I sigh feeling more and more frustrated. Just by the way he says my name tells me that they've been talking about me already, and the thought sends chills down my spine.

Tyler looks at me and winks, although he's so drunk it makes him teeter to the side and nearly fall into the fire. Please let him be the idiot who does it, I think to myself.

"You have a drink?" he slurs as he leans in toward me.

"Yep," I answer, holding up my beer.

"Let's go for a walk," he says as he closes in. His hands caress my hair but he's actually kind of pulling it when I think he means to just brush his fingers through it.

"I'm good here," I answer. Grant and Natalie are fully making out on the log behind me now, so it's just me and drunk Tyler.

"Come on," he says, and his hands snake around my waist and pinches my hip. He's leaning in, and although he's not quite as drunk as Grant, he still reeks of beer and something skunky.

He pulls me toward him, and he's surprisingly so strong I sort of stumble. I didn't expect it, so when he's not balanced enough to support himself or me, we both fall. I manage to catch myself before I completely hit the ground, but he doesn't and he lands in the sand spilling his beer.

"You fucking whore," he says with a laugh.

"I'm gonna go," I answer and turn to walk away.

As soon as I turn, I spot a familiar face across the fire. Piercing sky blue eyes and wavy brown locks. Even in this dark night, I can see the colorful designs on his skin, and they are the only beautiful thing in this scenario, like they truly do not belong here. I stop in my tracks as our eyes meet. His expression is harsh. Every feature of his face seems tight and laser focused on me.

Just as I'm about to take another step around the fire, I feel an arm around my waist again and a warm breath in my ear. "You're mine tonight."

I shove away from Tyler, and again he pulls me closer, this time trying to pull me out of the crowd and toward the darkness of the beach. A moment's panic sets in when I realize that if no one helps me, he might actually be strong enough to pull me away. He's twice my size, and even drunk he's far stronger than I am. My heart hammers in my chest as I try to squirm out of his grasp.

"Where are you going?" he slurs as he pulls harder.

I'm about to scream for help, but the panic makes me freeze up. What if no one cares? What if they're all so drunk or just so used to this kind of behavior that they do nothing at all? What if this guy actually pulls me into the darkness and has his way with me?

But before I can even react, there is a hand fisted in Tyler's collar. It forces him away so quickly, that he lets me go instantly. I watch as Tyler crumples to the ground like a wet rag. It happens so fast that I don't even notice who the angry fist is attached to. I'm suddenly overwhelmed by the buzz from the beer, the crackling fire, and the noisy thrumming of my pulse in my ears.

"She doesn't want to go with you," the voice booms as I turn to see Logan standing next to me, a furious sneer on his face.

Tyler jumps up surprisingly quickly to face Logan. "Who asked you, bro?" he says, huffing his wide nostrils in Logan's face.

"I see you push around any girl here like that again, I'll bury your ass in the fucking sand." Logan isn't as heated as Tyler. In fact, he seems cool, yet stern. The look of sheer intensity in his eyes is enough to make Tyler hesitate.

"You're just a piece of local trash," Tyler argues.

Logan ignores Tyler's lame insult as he touches the back of my arm and says, "Let's go." I turn my head to look at him, still surprised that he's here, that he defended me and possibly saved my life.

He must notice my frozen hesitation. "You don't want to stay here..." He says it like a question, and it doesn't take me long before I'm silently shaking my head.

"I'll give you a ride, let's go." His hand is touching the back of my arm again, not grabbing or pushing, but protecting me. Guiding me through the crowd in a way that says, "She's with me." And even though I was just in what could have been the worst scenario of my life, I can't help but feel almost excited about his subtle touch.

"You're going with him? Then you must be a piece of shit too!" Tyler calls after us.

"Keep going," Logan whispers as we walk.

Natalie is nice enough to come up for air long enough to ask me if I'm okay as I pass her. I don't even answer. She must notice Logan because she breathes a surprised "hey" toward him.

As soon as we're out of the crowd, it feels instantly silent and cold. I wrap my arms around myself as we approach the motionless street. Something warm covers my shoulders as I glance toward Logan. He's setting his black leather jacket across my body, instantly covering me in warmth.

"It'll be even colder on the bike," he says, but his words don't register.

I look back toward the party, but no one even looks toward us or comes after me. No one here cares about me at all. The thought chills me, so I squeeze his jacket tighter around me.

"Are you okay?" he asks.

"What was I thinking? I should have never been out there with him in the first place. This is all my fault." I press my face into my hands, letting the words tumble out of my mouth. I feel like such an idiot.

"Hey, hey," he says as he places his large hands on my shoulders, putting his face in front of mine, forcing me to look at him. "Can I call someone for you? Take you home?"

"No," I answer in a rush. I'd rather go back to that party, if we're being honest. My parents wouldn't notice anything was wrong or if they did, they would find some way to blame it on me.

"I only have my bike. Do you want me to get you out of here?" His voice is steady and full of confidence and concern. I look into his eyes and latch on to the intensity like a life raft and let the security I find there pull me to shore.

"Yes, please."

I let him guide me farther up the street toward where a motorcycle is parked in an empty lot. The shaking in my bones won't subside, and the anticipation of sitting on the back of a motorcycle only makes it worse.

He holds me by the hand and steadies me as I straddle one leg over the bike. "Be careful. The exhaust right here is really hot," he says as he points to a big silver pipe on the side.

"Thank you," I mumble.

He holds the handlebars of the bike as he steps over in front me, straightening it and making me latch my arms around his waist. My breath hitches as the deafening roar of the engine rumbles through my body.

And suddenly we're moving. I'm still holding tightly to his waist, but the more we move, the more my body relaxes against his. Leaning through the turns and accelerating down the street feels like we're flying together. The humming power between my legs ignites a heat there that makes me suddenly feel powerful and alive.

We ride for longer than I expect, and it doesn't take me long to realize that I don't need to hold so tightly to his waist. Our bodies move together as the bike carries us, our balance meeting in the middle keeping us in place through the stops and turns.

This is surreal. I'm on the back of his motorcycle. My boy, the one I've waited years to finally talk to. He's here, and my body is pressed up against his.

I lean my cheek against his back and let my arms ease their grasp. My fingers are gentle against his stomach as I feel his tight muscles through his thin T-shirt. I can feel him tense under my touch as we glide along together through the night, and it starts to feel as if with every mile we take together, we're erasing the darkness of what just happened on the beach.

Chapter Three

LOGAN

Her tight grip around my waist has me distracted. New riders always think they have to squeeze onto the person in front of them on a motorcycle, but when she clutched onto my body, I figured it was about more than the motorcycle.

Shit, I don't know how to handle a girl who's just been manhandled by a drunk pig. I couldn't even imagine. What I do know is that I could easily drop her off and go back to find that punk and pummel his face into the concrete to see how he likes to be treated like shit.

But I could tell by her response that she doesn't want

to go home, and I'm not about to leave her alone somewhere. So I take a scenic drive around the island. There's only one main roadway between mainland and Wickett, so as long as I avoid that, we could drive around this seven-mile island all night long. It never gets old.

When I feel her body relax and her cheek press up against my back, I know the ride is doing its job. Whenever I need to escape my problems, hopping on a bike has always done the trick for me. The wind, the rush, the vibrations of the motor between my legs... it's intoxicating.

Her fingers start to graze my stomach, and I can't decide if I don't ever want to get off this bike or if I want to stop it immediately and let her fingers graze as much as she wants.

No. That's a fucking dickhead thing to even think. After what this girl has been through tonight, she doesn't need a "piece of shit local" like me trying to lay the moves on too.

But I do know of a perfect place to stop. There's a quiet corner of the beach that is reserved only for the locals, but I happen to know all of the old hippies that live permanently here on the island, and they let me hang out on the beach anytime I want. It's the only place to escape the crowds during the busy season. And even better, most of them are out of town this week. If they don't own a business on the island, it's just better for them to avoid spring break altogether.

Can't say I blame them.

When I pull into the quiet cul-de-sac, I park my bike and kick out the stand to lean it up near the old wooden rails.

"Where are we?" she asks, looking around at the old homes and trailers grouped together on the street.

"It's a local neighborhood. A lot quieter over here. Is this okay?"

She looks around, and I see a smile creep onto her face. "It's so cute."

"I figured you might want something quiet." And it is quiet, completely silent, in fact. There are subtle streetlights and giant trees with hanging moss coating the street in a light warmth.

"I'm actually house-sitting for this guy here," I say, pointing to one of the small craftsmen at the corner. "Want me to run in and grab you a drink?"

"Do you live here?" she asks.

"I wish. Don't move. I'll be right back," I say as I run into the house. It doesn't take me long to find a couple beers and a few beach blankets resting on the chairs by the back door. Beach dwellers always have the good stuff.

As I run back outside, I notice that my arms are shaking. Nothing obvious, but coming from deep within my muscles. I haven't had a cigarette since I was at the shop. That must be it. I could have one now, but I can wait.

"Here you go," I say as I hand her a cold beer and toss

the blanket over my shoulder. "I just realized I don't even know your name."

"It's Sierra," she says with a smile. "And thank you." She holds up the drink, but her smile fades as she clutches the bottle to her chest.

"Are you doing okay?"

"I'm fine. Thank you. That was really nice of you. You don't have to take care of me like this."

"You said you didn't want to go home. I'm not going to just leave you somewhere." I crack open my beer and take a long sip. She does the same. Even though it's a little chilly at night, the cool carbonation calms my nerves.

"So you're going to spend your evening hanging out with me? Don't you have somewhere better to be?"

I cock my head in her direction. "Please."

She smiles. "What were you doing at that party anyway?"

"I could ask you the same thing," I reply, avoiding her question.

She lets out a deep sigh and rests against the wooden rail that leads to the water. "I was told it would be fun. I guess I didn't take into consideration who I was talking to."

I nod and am about to reply when I feel my phone buzz in my pocket. I don't need to check it. I know it's Hale. I completely forgot that I was supposed to be unloading this pocketful of eight balls to those punks at the bonfire.

Shit. I have over four ounces in my pocket as we speak. She doesn't deserve this, to be around me when I'm carrying so much. Nothing is going to happen, but God forbid I get caught, she would get pinned too, just for associating with me. I need to get rid of it, fast.

It's a dumb thing to do, but I'll stash it in the storage pocket of my bike while she isn't looking. She takes a small walk around the street corner to see some of the houses. When her back is turned, I ditch the package. I go ahead and stash my phone too. I don't want to hear anymore shit from Hale, and I'd like to pretend for a moment that he doesn't exist.

SIERRA

"Want to go for a walk?" he says as he raises his hand toward the beach. "It's really quiet out here. No bonfires or crowds."

I nod, squeezing his jacket around my body. It smells like leather and sea air. There's a hint of smoke there too, but I find the combination warm and comforting.

"Do you want your jacket back?" I ask, hoping he'll let me keep it on.

"No, it looks better on you anyway." He walks toward the beach without letting me see his smile as he says that. It's a sweet compliment but it almost feels like a fact coming from his mouth. Like he doesn't intend to make me feel better with the compliment.

"Thanks," I whisper as I follow him over the sandy planks that connect the street to the beach. Once we reach the sand, my breath is caught in my throat. It is so gorgeous out here. The only light is the moon and it shimmers against the surface of the ocean like a lightbulb.

"It's beautiful," I murmur.

"I know, right?" he says. He flips off his boots and shoves his socks into them, so I follow suit, leaving my white Chucks sitting next to his black shoes. He's in tight black jeans and a snug-fitting white V-neck T-shirt. I can see the muscles in his arms through the fabric, and I almost wish we were still on the bike so I have a reason to cling to him.

We make our way down toward the shore so that we can walk on the firm, wet sand instead of the loose dry beach. It's easier to walk and the cool water on my feet feels refreshing.

"Are you from Wickett?"

"Born and raised," he says.

"Really? You're lucky."

"Hardly," he answers. "Don't get me wrong, it's a nice place to grow up, but not when you're in foster care. I spent about six years on the mainland in a nice home, but I aged out and came back here to work with my brother."

"Oh. Is that other tattoo artist your brother?" I ask, drawn into his story.

"Murph? No. He was my brother's best friend, but my brother died a year ago."

He says everything so matter-of-factly. Foster system? Dead brother? How can he be so calm about it all? I want to touch him, hug him, but he doesn't look like he'd be very receptive to the contact.

"I'm so sorry," I say, but it doesn't feel like enough.

He smiles at me, lifting the corners of his mouth and looking at me as he runs his hands through his hair. Out at the shore, it's even darker so I can barely see him.

I know that I should probably avoid walking in dark remote areas with a stranger, especially after what just almost happened to me, but I trust him for reasons I can't explain. First, he did save me, so that's a point in his favor. But it's more than that. He's nice to me without reason, and even though this is the first conversation we've had, it feels like I've known him for years.

"Are you sure you don't have anywhere else to be? I feel bad that you're stuck hanging out with me?"

He laughs, a low rumble from his chest. His hands are shoved into his pockets while he walks. "You're kidding, right?"

"I'm serious."

"I don't mind," he reassures me as he places a hand on my shoulder. "It's my pleasure, seriously."

We walk in silence together with only the sound of the waves to serenade us. The spot where he touched my shoulder is humming from the contact. I want him to touch me again. Visions of him turning toward me, kissing me, pinning me to the sand and groaning into my neck as we climax together...

I swallow down the filthy vision. For a virgin, I tend to have a lot of thoughts like that. With everyone. The cute boy bagging my groceries. The guy who cleans my parents' pool. Even the waiter at the upscale restaurant we go to at least once a week.

These dirty thoughts are my secret. As far as I know, they're normal, but I would never tell anyone about them. It's not like I'm trying to hang on to my virginity forever, but I just keep waiting for the person who will make all the visions go away. Someone who will fill my imagination for me.

"So what college do you go to?" he asks. It's a small talk question, and I hope he doesn't think he has to keep up boring conversation for me. I quite enjoy the silence anyway.

"I don't go to college," I answer.

He stops walking and stares at me with a worried expression. "How old are you?" he deadpans.

I can't help but laugh, barreled over with my hands on my knees. "I'm nineteen!"

He laughs too, but it's a hesitant chuckle. "When you said you weren't in college..."

"I'm not in high school!" I answer. "I just meant that

I took a year off before going to college."

"Oh, thank fuck."

He resumes his walking and we keep pace together. "How old are you?" I ask.

"Twenty-five," he answers.

I can feel the beat of my heart pick up speed when I look at him. Twenty-five. Just as I expected. He has a youthful face with the demeanor of someone wiser and harder, like he's been through a lot. It's heartbreaking and somehow painfully beautiful.

LOGAN

Her perfect pink toes in the sand have my attention throughout most of our walk. I keep my eyes glued, even in the dark, on her delicate features in the moonlight. I have to shove my hands in my pockets to stop myself from touching her blonde locks, her soft skin, the thin layers that hide what I'm sure is a perfect body.

That white T-shirt she's wearing hangs off of her shoulders and the soft rise of her chest. And the way she looks with my jacket across her shoulders has me feeling breathless. But as much as I love the way she looks in it, I can't help but imagine pushing it off of her so that I can slip my fingers under her shirt and around her soft tits.

God, I'm disgusting.

We stop after about an hour of walking to sit on the beach and stare out at the waves. "Don't your parents worry about you?" I ask.

"Not here. They encourage me to engage in spring break behavior at Wickett. Like they want me to get it outta my system here. I think that's what everyone does. It's kinda gross if you think about it."

"Trust me, I do. The locals can't help but support the spring breakers, because we need the business, but at the same time..."

"Yeah, I get it."

"But you're not like them," I say, looking over at those perfect pink toes digging into the sand.

"I hope not," she answers with a smile.

"What do these mean?" she asks as she traces her fingers across the skin of my arms.

"Nothing really," I say through a tight throat. Her fingers on my skin are awakening something in me that I don't really want to wake right now. I glance down at the part of my bicep that she's touching. It's the galaxy part of my sleeve with a swirl of purple, pink, and blue. I wanted as little black in my tatts as possible; I had enough darkness in my life. I wanted something bright on the outside.

"It's so beautiful. I can hardly see it in the moonlight."

"I'll be happy to show you more another time," I say, and it slips out of my mouth without bypassing my brain. Instantly, she blushes and presses her lips together, creating little dimples in her cheeks. "Oh shit...that's not what I meant." I'm trying to dig myself out of what sounded like a terrible pickup line, but it's not working.

She laughs silently, looking at my forearm as if she's ignoring what I said. Or maybe she's secretly hoping that I meant it the way it sounded. Now she has my arm in her hands, looking through the blue and pink flowers there. I'm watching her face. She really is the most beautiful girl that's ever touched my arm, and she's far too pretty for me. Too clean. Too pure.

Is she really into a guy like me? If she knew the dark things that went through my head, she wouldn't be interested for long. I could scare her away in one thought.

"I like this one," she says, pressing her fingers along the orchid near my wrist. I keep my hand relaxed as she holds my wrist, but my fingers are so close to her body that I can feel them humming. I could outstretch my digits and touch her stomach. Push her against the sand and pull that soft pink skirt above her hips.

"Thanks," I whisper.

Her eyes rise up to meet mine through hooded lashes, and I can feel the heat coming from her skin like a flame. She wants me. It's in that look. She wants my dirty hands and dirty thoughts to cover her like a roaming storm—and I want it too. I want to feel her soft breasts under my palms. I want to taste the sweetness between her legs. I want it so bad, but I can't.

Something holds me back.

And it's calling me from my pockets like a little reminder that I'm not good enough. I'm wasted. Broken. I can't be with beautiful girls or make anyone happy because I belong to something else. Not whole enough to even give her the pleasure I so badly want to.

Her fingers are still on my arm and her thumb is still lightly pressed against the pulse on my wrist. I know she can feel it under my skin, beating faster with each second.

"I should get you back home," I say, breaking the stare and looking toward the ocean. Her perfect pink toes catch my attention again. I would be a criminal to even lay a finger on her. Or in her.

"I'm not in any hurry," she says, tucking her blonde strands behind her ear. I can see her blushing. She's not used to this kind of thing, I can tell. Fuck, she might even be a virgin.

My cock reacts to that thought. To be the first inside her. I have to swallow down that desire, but it's not easy.

Why the fuck would she want someone like me?

A thrill ride during her naughty spring break, I remind myself. Of course. That's what all the rich girls want while they're here. A quick, dirty romp. I could give it to her. I could make her come right here under the moon until she can't take anymore.

No, you can't, the voice in my pocket reminds me.

"It's getting late," I say. My voice is gravel from the restraint.

"Okay," she mumbles, looking at me with uncertainty. Dammit. She thinks I don't want her.

Good. Let her think I'm a dickhead. It's better for everyone that way.

I stand up and pull her to her feet. She hops up inches away from my body and I pull away, afraid she might feel the stiffness in my jeans, but she stares up at me with those sweet baby blues, and I want to attack her mouth with mine. I want to bite her lips and nibble at her neck, but I press out a deep sigh and turn back toward the way we came. The sooner she and I get vertical and moving, the better.

The walk back is quiet, but I can feel her presence next to me. When we get to the bike, I help her climb back on and let her put her arms around me again when I get in front of her. This time, her soft hands are pressed against my chest, then my arms, and my legs. She's doing this on purpose, and it's driving me nuts. It takes everything in me not to stop this bike.

When she tells me her condo building, I realize it's not far from where we're at. I don't know if that's a good thing or not. I should be relieved, but I don't want her to peel her body from mine. Where did this girl come from?

I pull up to her building and let the bike rumble in

neutral while she gets off. "Thank you again," she says as she looks at me, curling her hair behind her ears again. "I had a really nice time, and you didn't have to do that."

"My pleasure," I answer, but I keep my face cold and blank. The effort it takes to keep my hands to myself is excruciating.

Then she does something I don't expect. She leans in for a hug, wrapping her arms around my neck, and I breathe in the flowery scent of her hair as she holds herself against me, longer than I think most hugs should be.

As she pulls away, she stops and lets her lips touch mine. It's not a sexual kiss, but a soft acknowledgement that we should be touching. It's her way of saying that this is what we could be doing—and so much more—if I wasn't holding myself back. I don't even kiss her back, and before I can even react, her lips are gone. She walks away without a word, still wearing my jacket.

I ride for another twenty minutes, taking a long ride around the island, thinking about that kiss. How in just a few hours, this girl has turned my world upside down. How I want to drive back to that apartment and knock on every door until I find her. How I want to press my lips against hers before ripping her clothes off and burying myself in her, never pulling out.

I pass the spot where the party was, just to see who is left, but the fire is gone, nothing but a smoky breeze drifting off to sea. A few people are still there, mostly making out, and from the looks of it, fucking lazily on the beach.

It's too late to make any sales, so I move on. Parking at the spot in front of the shop, I walk toward the door and stop. I feel the little baggie in my pocket, and it's still calling to me, but the voice sounds different now. The thought of letting myself go there makes me want to punch something hard. I don't want to phase out, in search of some bliss that could never match the possibility of what I felt tonight. I can't let my mind near the idea of dumping those little white crystals into the pipe and the beautiful burn when the flame hits the glass.

Instead, I turn and walk straight back to the beach. Standing near the water's edge, now so much farther up the beach than before, I pull the small bag out of my pocket. I just think about her lips against my mouth. We could have this and so much more.

I should have dumped it. I wanted to so much, no matter how much it fucking hurt. I wanted to dump it and never get high again.

But I didn't. Because it called to me, begged me to stay, promised me the comfort I needed. So rather than let myself dream of Sierra and the possibility of what we could have, I avoided thinking of her at all. I couldn't let her and this addiction coexist in my mind.

And since I couldn't lose myself in her tonight, I lost myself in something far worse.

Chapter four

SIERRA

My parents are golfing with their island friends. This is what they do every year on Wickett. They leave me and expect me to cling onto some random friends and never really show my face at the condo. It's our little deal that I never agreed to. They take me to the beach, and I leave them alone.

I sleep in late because it took me hours to fall asleep last night. I didn't sneak in until after three, but then I tossed and turned in my bed thinking about Logan's arm in my hand. Those dirty thoughts kept me from sleep. Why didn't he touch me? Did I make myself look too desperate? Am I just a young, horny rich girl to him? He probably has plenty of beautiful women at his feet. Why would he waste his time on a girl like me?

The cleaning ladies work around me as I mope my way through the kitchen in my cami and pajama shorts. It's after lunch by the time I finally get dressed and out the door. I throw a short sundress over my bikini and toss my hair up in a messy bun. I drape Logan's jacket around my shoulders as I walk.

I don't have a real destination in mind, but I feel myself drawn toward the tattoo shop like a beacon. I'll just stop in to say hello, give him his jacket back, and offer to pay him back with dinner. Real slick, Sierra.

As I walk down the busy boardwalk, I remember the bookstore I used to go to when I was younger. It used to have bright window displays and a warm dusty ambiance inside—books stacked on the stairs and in piles all over the small space. I hadn't been the past couple years, mostly because I was too busy pining for a certain elusive tattoo artist.

I have plenty of time today, so I take a quick detour to stop in. There are heavy bells on the door that clang as I let it close behind me. "Good morning," a small voice calls.

"Good morning," I answer, although I don't see the person I'm responding to.

The bookstore hasn't changed much, except that it's far dustier and the display window is filled with old books, cleaning supplies, and worn-out signs.

Movement catches my eye when I spot an old woman trying to move a box onto a table. I rush over to get it from her. "I've got that," I say as I lift it for her.

"Thank you, dear."

After a quick glance at the old woman, I'm shocked to see that it's the same old owner that I remember from my childhood. She must be over seventy by now. Looking around at the mess of the store, I find it hard to believe that she runs this place by herself.

"Please have a look around," she says in a sing-song tone. She has a warm smile and unkempt gray curls.

"I remember coming here when I was a kid," I explain. I don't know why I feel compelled to tell her that, but it just slips out.

"Oh yeah?" she answers with a smile. "It was much better when my husband was still alive. Now, it's just me." She's dusting the shelves with an old feather duster, but I think she might just be making it worse.

"It's a lovely store," I lie. It used to be a lovely store. How she keeps it open I have no idea.

"Thank you, dear."

Standing between two shelves at the front of the store, I gaze at the window and let myself imagine how I would make it look if I could decorate it. Beach reads. Some color and window decals to draw the eye in. If people came to the beach, they would want a book to take with them. I could even put a little beach chair up there with a few different books and a little fake margarita. Maybe even a cute letter board sign with a funny slogan to draw people in.

I pick out four books. I don't need four books this week, but I feel bad and want to bring her some business. I can't shake the feeling that I could do so much more.

LOGAN

Hale is banging on the back door. It's past three, which means he's here to pick up his money from what I sold last night. I groan thinking about that little punk sitting outside. I didn't sell anything last night, and I really don't want to deal with his shit about it.

I'm going to just give him the package back and tell him to fuck off. I've been wanting to tell him that anyway. Of course, I don't feel the same resounding clarity that I felt last night.

I slept like shit last night. No matter how hard I tried not to think about Sierra after getting high, the guilt kept me up until almost dawn. When I finally drifted off, I dreamt of her pink toes in the sand and her legs wrapped around my waist.

When I woke up this morning, I decided I was done with getting high. But mostly done with selling. I won't belong to Hale anymore. I only owe him a few hundred, and I have that on me so I would pay him and be done with it.

Even as I run out to the bike to get the package out of the side pouch, I start to feel less sure. Somehow to my warped mind, staying high is the easier option. I'm an addict, and my brother was an addict, and if he couldn't keep his shit together, what's the point of me even trying? I pull out a cigarette to steady my nerves.

Then something black and white catches my eye in the shop two doors down. It's the old bookstore that never gets any business. Maybe they're finally cleaning it out. But then I spot something familiar. It's my jacket. Then her long blonde hair. She's rearranging the window display. A bright smile on her face as she places a stack of books on the platform by the door, I smile seeing her helping the old woman working there.

She catches sight of me. I'm standing outside by my bike, ready to grab the package, when she sends me a warm smile and a small wave. The brief memory of her lips on mine suddenly comes back, and I nearly forget why I feel so irritated and anxious today. The only thing I want to get high on now is those lips.

I wave back and hear Murph yell from inside the shop. "Hey, Logan, come take care of this punk before I kill him!"

"I'm coming!" I holler back. I lift the flap on my bike's pouch and reach in for the package. But it's too flat. There's nothing in there. My heart stops beating as I root through the side pouch like it's suddenly going to appear in the shallow pocket.

"Fuck!" I say. I rack my brain. I didn't bring it up-
stairs last night. I didn't. Like a fucking idiot, I left
it out here. I didn't want it in my apartment because
I knew I wouldn't be able to control myself. "Fuck,
fuck, fuck!"

I turn around and run into the shop. "Murph, have
you seen a brown package anywhere? Did I bring it
in?"

"Jesus fuck, Logan. What did you do?"

"Did you see it?" I shout. I'm getting erratic and I
know that Murph would knock me out before he'd
deal with any of this shit, but he doesn't. He shakes
his head and stomps to the back alley.

"Get the fuck out here before I call the cops," he
bellows at Hale. I don't let him see me in the shop as
I rummage through the drawers and cabinets behind
the front counter.

"You don't want cops at your shop, Murph," Hale says
back. That kid has a lot of balls to talk to Murph like
that. The shop owner is 6'5" and looks like he could
break the white-collar drug dealer like a twig.

"If you don't get the fuck out of here, it'll be an ambulance," Murph yells back.

"You tell Logan that he owes me seven grand!" he says

Murph doesn't answer as he lets the door slam shut.
When he passes me, he mumbles, "Deal with this."

I don't answer him. I just run up the stairs to the
apartment above and start to rummage through my

tiny one-room studio. I've been renting the place above the tattoo shop. It was my brother's before, so Murph doesn't charge me much and doesn't complain when I cause trouble. I owe him my life, and this is how I repay him. "Fuck, fuck, fuck."

The bag isn't there. I knew it wouldn't be. The stunning realization of the fact I've been avoiding comes crashing down on me. The drugs were stolen. Not surprisingly. I should have never left them in the bike. But I'm a weak fuck-up and couldn't have them in my apartment without smoking it all to death. Fuck.

When I come back downstairs, Murph is waiting for me. He doesn't have another appointment until five, so the shop is empty and quiet. "You lose something?" he asks with his broad arms crossed over his chest.

"I try to do something right and this is what happens," I mumble with my face in my hands.

"Don't start that shit. You screwed up, so you have to deal with it."

"I need to get out of here," I say as I reach for my keys out of my pocket. Just as I start toward the door, she's standing there. In a short white sundress with my black jacket over the top. She looks like someone out of a magazine. Not someone who belongs in a tattoo shop with a junkie like me.

She smiles at me as she pulls open the door. I want to see her, but I don't know if I can face her right now. My hands are balled into fists.

"Shake it off," Murph says as he turns toward her. He

greets her with a fake smile.

"Hi," she says with a glowing expression as she walks up the counter. "Hi, Logan," she says to me. Murph turns toward me with a look of shock on his face. That had to be the last thing he expected her to say.

"I just wanted to bring back your jacket," she explains.

I walk up to the counter to face her. Murph retreats to the back of the shop to give us some privacy. I couldn't fake a smile if I tried, and I feel terrible for the tense, cold expression on my face.

"You can keep it," I say. "It looks better on you, anyway." I try to busy myself with cleaning up around the front counter so that I don't have to look at her blue eyes and the look of sweet innocence there. She would be better off leaving me alone and getting as far as possible.

"I couldn't. This is a nice jacket," she says.

It is a nice jacket. My brother bought it for me. As a celebration after my first tattoo and, I suspect, as a way to induct me into his motorcycle club. But I don't want it back now. It will only remind me of her. And my brother, for that matter. And I don't want to be reminded of either of them.

"I want to thank you again for everything last night," she says. She's trying to get my attention, to prolong our interaction, and I'm the biggest dickhead for ignoring her and trying to push her away. But she needs to go. And far.

"It was nothing," I say.

"It was definitely not nothing," she argues through an awkward laugh.

I don't answer and she stands there, her smile fading away. She glances back at Murph who's cleaning and organizing supplies.

"Maybe we could hang out later. I'd love another ride on your bike."

"I work pretty late tonight. Spring break is busy for us."

"I'll wait." She really won't give up. No matter how much I just wish she would leave, even though I know my world will be a great deal darker when she's not standing here in front of me. She can sense my hesitation.

"You're the nicest person to me on this whole island, and I thought we had a nice time." She's whispering so that Murph can't hear.

I swallow down the urge to tell her that last night was one of the best nights I've had in a long time. I want to tell her that I'll quit it all because of her. That I want to stay with her everyday so that I never light up again. That she is my new addiction.

But I don't.

"Sierra, you don't need to be hanging out with me."

"So I should be hanging out with guys like Tyler instead?" she asks as she tucks her hair behind her ears.

"Fuck no." I say it a little too loud. Murph stops what he's doing for a second but quickly resumes.

"Do you have a girlfriend?" she asks.

"No. I'm just not the right guy for you, Sierra."

Damn, this hurts. This is so hard I'd rather punch my hand through the glass case before saying something like that to her again. Her demeanor changes instantly. She thinks I'm not interested in her. Couldn't be farther from the fucking truth. I want her so bad that I want to kick my own ass for turning her down, but I have to. I have to push her away instead of pushing her against this wall and put my hands under that white sundress. Hearing her say my name as I make her come right here in the shop in the middle of the day.

One glimpse into my twisted mind would send her running.

"I get it," she says as she steps away.

Then she peels my jacket off her shoulders, and it physically hurts to watch.

"I shouldn't keep this," she says as she smacks it against the counter and turns without a word to walk out of the shop and out of my life.

That's it, baby girl. Keep going. Don't look back.

Chapter five

SIERRA

I'm a mixture of angry, sad, and confused. How could we have had such a nice time last night and today it's a different story? God, I'm such an idiot. I kissed him, thinking he would be interested, but I get nothing in return. I'm too innocent for him. Too young. Too inexperienced.

I'm flooded with self-deprecating thoughts like: why would a guy like him want a girl like me? I bet he could get anyone he wants.

I keep moving, trying to walk out the way I'm feeling with every step, but it's not working. The farther

I get from that shop, the worse I feel. I want to turn around and beg him to give me a chance. That's not like me. I don't beg guys for anything. Not that I have a ton of experience with guys, but I've had a few interactions—nothing farther than second base—and it was enough to know that I never had to really ask. They were always willing.

When I turn toward the large boardwalk and the pavilion over the beach, I hear a familiar voice. By the time I notice Natalie, Grant, and Tyler, as well as a few people I don't know, it's too late to turn back. I can tell the exact moment they recognize me, so I pick up speed, hoping to get lost in the crowd toward the end of the pier.

"Where's your friend?" Grant calls after me.

Natalie tries to shush him, but she's laughing too, so he's not taking her very seriously.

One of them runs over to me.

"Leave me alone," I call back without turning, but it doesn't stop him. Before I know it, there's an arm around my shoulder.

"Hey, baby, we got off on the wrong foot last night. Think we can start over?" Tyler says as he walks with me.

"Get off of me," I say as I try to shove him away. He laughs it off, making the entire scenario seem like two friends messing around. No one around us even reacts.

"You're gonna hang out with us tonight, right, baby?"

He's pulling me closer, and it's making my stomach turn.

"I'm going to scream," I say. I really don't want to make a big deal out of it. It wouldn't be that hard to really cause a scene and get people's attention, but I just want him to leave me alone before it comes to that.

"Hey, stop," he says. "Why do you hate me so much? Come on, give me a chance." His head is cocked to the side and he keeps his hands on my shoulders. It's such a typical reaction. To play the victim and act like I'm the one on the attack. Like I'm being unfair to him. I'm not falling for it for one second, but when I turn toward Natalie and Grant, they're looking at us, waiting for me to smile or act like everything is okay. And for one second, I actually consider it.

"I'm not the right girl for you," I say as I try to walk away.

"Hey, baby, it's not that serious. We just wanna have some fun. Don't you want to have some fun? Come on, please?" he begs, putting his hands together and literally dropping to his knees. And fuck me, I'm actually breaking into a smile. I shake my head at him.

"See you later," I say as I turn and walk away.

He doesn't respond as he walks back to the group, and I hear them all give out a collective "awww" when he rejoins them.

The fact that he played me so good that I almost gave in makes me even more angry. Last night, he was so wasted that he could have done serious damage to me, physically and emotionally, and he never apologized for it. And yet, Logan thinks he's not good enough for me. It's so unfair and makes zero sense to me.

I grab an iced coffee from one of the vendors on the pier before sitting down in the shade with my phone to do a little reading. When I walk back toward land, the group is gone.

There's a small crosswalk that leads from the beach side of the street to the stores on the other side. After pushing the button to cross, someone standing on the other side catches my eye. He's tall, blond, and has a charming smile which he's pointing directly at me. I feel myself blush as he stares at me.

When the light turns, he doesn't cross but shuffles around in place as if he's contemplating whether to cross or not. I give him a gentle smile as I walk toward him, and when it appears like he's waiting for me, I stop on the other side, looking at him expectantly.

"I was gonna cross, but then realized that I needed to stop and say something to you."

"Okay," I blush.

"A girl as pretty as you shouldn't be walking alone."

I shake my head, feeling awkward. Other people at the crosswalk are now looking at me, and I'm feeling desperate to get away from so much attention.

"Can I walk with you?" he says.

"Oh, I was just heading back home."

He puts his hands up in surrender. "I won't follow

you home or try to make any creepy moves. Just let me get to know you."

After getting turned down by Logan and nearly convinced to hang out with Tyler, I'm feeling desperate for normal human interaction. So, I agree to let him walk with me. He is really good-looking and has a sincere smile.

"Are you going this way?" he asks, pointing toward the shops that lead to my apartment.

"Yes," I nod.

Then without saying anything, he gestures for me to walk, and I let him stay next to me.

"Where are your friends?" he asks.

"Everyone I've met so far have been total jerks," I say as I curl my hair behind my ears.

"No way. Jerks to you?"

"Yeah, long story." I roll my eyes.

"I'm sorry. That's terrible. Did you go to the bonfire last night?"

"Yes."

He shakes his head. "Yeah, that was your mistake. Nothing but a bunch of drunk idiots there."

"Tell me about it," I laugh.

"And I assume your parents brought you to Wickett for spring break..." He looks at me with raised eyebrows.

"How did you guess?"

"I'm used to it."

"Are you a local?" I ask.

"Yeah, why?"

I look at him, but it's not registering. He doesn't look like a local.

"No reason," I say. I realize that we are coming up to the tattoo shop, and we're going to walk right in front of the window. Logan might see us walking together, and I use the opportunity to make him jealous. So as we approach, I make sure to find whatever this new guy is saying very funny and even touch his arm as we pass. Out of the corner of my eye, I see someone standing behind the counter, someone that's definitely not the big, burly bearded man.

LOGAN

I don't want to take any clients today, but at this point, I can't afford not to. I haven't heard from Hale since he was here banging on the door, but I'm expecting that he'll be here for his money any minute.

After finishing up a couple easy black line tatts for a small group of college kids, I stand in the front of the shop waiting for the night rush. It's still late afternoon, but it'll get crazy after dinner time.

My brain is still replaying the terrible way I treated Sierra earlier today. The look she had on her face as she walked away, without my black jacket hanging off her bare shoulders, will stay etched in my memory forever. I wanted to run after her so fucking bad. Cover her with more than just my jacket.

And just like that, the two people I can't get out of my head appear all at once. Sierra is walking in front of the shop, but she's not alone. My next breath gets caught in my chest as I see her pass with Hale by her side. She's touching his arm, laughing, and he's laughing back. Just before they're out of my sight, Hale glances into the shop and stares at me straight in the eye.

What the fuck?

It's a coincidence. He can't possibly know about my connection with Sierra, but the idea of them together does not make me feel any better. Tyler was pretty bad, but he has nothing on Hale. All Hale cares about is money. And his avenue for more money is drugs. Plain and simple. I've seen him in action. He will do anything he has to do to move more drugs, to make more money—and that includes getting innocent newcomers hooked and pushing product for him.

"I'll be back," I say as I grab my keys.

"I have a client at six," Murph says as I walk out the front door. The pair are now too far down the street to see me, so I rush out to my bike and start up the engine. Going in the opposite direction, I turn on the narrow streets behind the row of shops, making my way toward where I remember dropping Sierra off the night before.

I'm not spying, but I just want to make sure she

doesn't do anything crazy like let him into her condo or let him know which unit is hers.

I pull into a spot at the back of the building and watch for the couple to walk into view. They won't notice me back here, but I am in a good position to see them.

It takes about ten more minutes before I hear their voices, walking through the parking lot toward the building.

They stop near a palm tree at the front. "Thanks for walking me," she says.

"Anytime," he answers. He's like a different person than the Hale I know. His voice sounds like it's drenched in syrup and fake with sweetness. "Can I call you?" he asks.

Don't give him your number, Sierra. Please, fuck, don't do it.

"Sure," she says with not nearly enough hesitation. She gives him her phone to put his number in. He quickly types his number before giving it back to her. Then his phone goes off with her text message.

"Awesome," he responds. "And you'll come to the party tonight?"

"Maybe," she says. She's trying to walk away, but he's being persistent.

"Please do." He's walking backward, away from where she's standing. "Goodbye, gorgeous."

"Bye," she says.

I watch him walk away, toward the main drag of the

boardwalk. I assume that Sierra is walking into her building through the front entrance, until I notice her walking toward me. She must be entering through the back entrance, and I have nowhere to hide as she approaches.

Chapter Six

SIERRA

"Logan?" I gasp as I turn the corner into the parking lot behind the condos. "What are you doing here?" I take a quick glance behind me to make sure that the new stranger—whose name I didn't catch—isn't within earshot. I have nothing to be ashamed about, but I can't help but feel a tinge of guilt about being seen with someone else.

"I...uh...felt bad for how I treated you earlier. I wanted to apologize." His voice is cold and forced.

"Oh..."

"And I saw you walking home with that guy. Do you

know who that is?" he asks, looking more angry than concerned.

"Um, no, actually. He just offered to walk me home."

"I'm sure he did," he says with a cold expression.

"Do you have a problem with that?" I try to walk past him. It's like I suddenly remember that I spent a couple hours with this guy, and he shut me down and has no hold over me whatsoever. I can walk with whomever I want.

Of course, none of this changes how badly I want him to kiss me or touch me.

"Yeah, you can't just walk around with strange guys. They only want one thing." He reaches out to hold my arm and keep me from walking inside.

As soon as his fingers wrap around my arm, I glare at him. "And what about you? What do you want?"

"I don't want to see a nice girl like you end up in a bad situation." I can feel his grip get tighter but not in a controlling way. He's restraining himself. I can feel it.

"What if I'm not such a nice girl?"

"I'm not buying it," he says without taking his eyes from mine.

"I thought you came here to apologize."

"That was until I saw you walking around with him."

I pull my arm away, in a dare. I dare him to grab it again. I dare him to hold me down. Pin me against this wall. Make me his and only his.

"Are you going to see him again?" he asks without any

hint of curiosity in his voice. We are not the same two people who sat on that beach last night. How quickly everything between us became so charged. It's like we've shared something intimate, and we're no longer strangers.

"He invited me to a party tonight."

"You can't go," he orders me. He seems almost desperate.

"Why not?"

"Because you'll be with me."

I stop where I stand on the first step leading up to the building doors. My chest is visibly heaving from my weighted breaths. There's nothing I want more right now than to spend my evening with him, but I can tell that there must be something more to this invitation.

"But you said—"

"I changed my mind. I was stupid to push you away."

I wait, watching him struggle through those two clumsy lines.

"Was that your version of an apology?" I ask.

He grits his teeth and I can see the flex in his jaw.

"I'm sorry. Please hang out with me tonight."

"Okay," I say. "I'll think about it." Then I turn and head up toward the apartment building, leaving him standing there without an answer, hopefully feeling as lost and desperate as I felt two hours ago.

LOGAN

This girl is impossible. Here I thought she was an innocent spring breaker, but I can already see the potential for her to really put me through hell. I'm glad she'll be with me tonight, but more than anything, I need to keep her as far away from Hale as possible. Whether he knows about her connection to me or not is not a risk I'm willing to take. I've pissed him off enough this weekend, so I don't need him taking that out on her.

In one week, she'll be gone, and I won't feel so responsible for keeping her safe. Then, I can really focus on getting clean...if that's what I choose to do by the end of the week. I have a bead of sweat on my forehead and an ache in my stomach that says otherwise.

I pull behind the shop to park my bike, and not surprisingly, Hale is waiting there for me. He has a completely different expression on his face than when I saw him ten minutes ago trying to sweet talk his way into Sierra's pants.

He almost always comes alone, which is surprising to me. How can this guy think he is so powerful and above the rest of us that he can just show up without any backup and think he's big enough to take me on? Because he sees me as a piece of shit addict who needs him too much. I can't fucking wait for that to change.

I scowl at him as I dismount the bike and walk over

with my shoulders back and my chest puffed. He won't intimidate me, and the more I think about him putting his hand on Sierra's back, the more I want to punch my fist through his face.

"Where the fuck is my money, Logan?" he says, lifting his chin toward me. I glance down at his coral-colored shorts and leather loafers, and I hate him even more for the way he can skate by any suspicion or trouble just because of how rich and perfect he looks.

"No one was buying," I say, flat and expressionless.

He narrows his eyes at me. "Then, give me back the product. Someone else is going to sell it."

"I can handle it."

"Are you fucking with me, Logan? Do you really think that's wise?" He steps toward me, a smug look on his face, and I can see his sandy-blond hair fall into his eyes.

"What are you going to do if I am, Hale?" It's a blatant threat and a stupid one. I'm a cornered animal, and my only line of defense is to attack, which never really works out for the prey.

Hale looks visibly stunned by my remark. He runs his hands through his hair, setting it back in its place, and actually lets out a hearty laugh. "Who do you think the cops will believe, Logan?" He takes a step toward me. "Aren't you on probation? All I have to do is put in a noise complaint and you're toast. And do you think they would ever listen to you in the first place? You're trash. Your brother and his friends were trash. This whole shop is trash, and you will end up where all trash ends up: dead or in jail. Do you have any idea the team of lawyers I have on my side? The money my father sinks into that police station. You have nothing, Logan."

My jaw clicks as I squeeze my teeth together with my fists clenched at my sides. I want to hit him so bad my arms are shaking, but everything he's saying is true. He has such a head start in this race that there is literally nothing I can do to catch up. One move and I'll end up in jail, end of story.

"You have until the end of the week, Logan. I want my seven grand, in cash. No product. You sell it all." He starts to turn away before he flips back toward me. "You know what...why don't you make it ten grand? And if I don't get my money by Sunday night, I'll go to the cops. I don't need you or the money. I just want you to remember who's on top around here, Logan."

Then, he walks away without another word.

I look down at my phone to see that it's nearly six, which means Murph is going to be busy with a client and hates being in the shop alone. I walk in the back and throw him an apology before walking up to the front to handle the few lingering customers, which consists of mostly college guys looking to get their frat signs on their backs or chests.

The ancient art of tattooing...now used to brand a stupid fucking club on your chest.

I'm in a foul mood for the next couple hours. All

I can think about is whether or not Sierra will go to that party with Hale and inevitably end up in a terrible situation or whether she'll come here to see me. I'm not going to make this about jealousy, but there is a part of me that wants to be sure it's me she wants, more than him.

All of that aside, I still have that one lingering issue of the ten thousand dollars I have to pay Hale in one week or face jail time. Which really should be the major issue on my mind, but all I can think about is her long blonde hair up in that ponytail and how it exposed the back of her neck and shoulders so that when she gave me that furious look today, all I could focus on was how perfect her skin shone in the afternoon sunlight.

I really should not be so obsessed with this girl right now. With so much on my plate and a royal fuck-up to fix, I can't be letting her get into my head.

But at the same time, I can't shake the feeling that this girl could be good for me. Not in the sense that she would save me or change me, but that she is the first person in a long time that I want to be better for. I don't want her hanging around people like Hale or Tyler. I want her safe in the arms of someone who she knows without a doubt would never hurt her, use her, or bring her any pain. And I know that I could be that person.

The old me would convince myself to just fuck her already to get her out of my head. If I'm so hungry for a taste, then I should just get my fill so that when she leaves in a week, I'm satisfied and can move on with my life.

But what life?

Suddenly, I have myself thinking about what kind of life I'd be living after this spring break is over. More drugs. More jail. More fights and mistakes and one-night stands.

I've never let myself imagine more, but when she's around...

The front door bells chime and I look up just in time to see her standing there. A thin yellow cardigan is buttoned around a blue dress that is cut a little lower than I would expect from her. I can see the soft curves of her breasts peeking out from the neckline.

When she sees me, she doesn't smile. Instead, she gives me a smug told-you-so look and walks up to the counter I'm leaning on. She places her elbows on the glass and our faces are so close, I could lean forward an inch and kiss her.

"What can I help you with?" I ask without giving away too much.

"I told you I would think about it, and I thought about it."

"And here you are."

"Here I am..." she says, her voice drifting.

"I get off in thirty minutes." I stand up, putting more distance between us before I do anything stupid.

"I can hang out," she answers as she walks around

the lobby, keeping her eyes on me and her fingers delicately brushing the countertop. She's toying with me, trying to make me crazy. It's working.

Chapter Seven

SIERRA

I love watching him work. The flexing muscles beneath the tattoos on his arms and shoulders is a show I would pay to see. I get to watch him pierce someone's nose, and the intense concentration on his face as he works is the sexiest thing I've ever admired.

It's almost ten by the time he is ready to leave. "Shit, it's late," he says as he glances up at the clock and says goodbye to the other man in the shop.

"It's okay," I say as we stroll outside. I'm silently praying that we have to take his motorcycle to wherever we are going.

"Are you hungry?" he asks.

"A little."

"I'm starving." Then, he looks at me as if he's mulling an idea over in his head. "There's a great food truck on the far side of the island. We could have a little picnic on the beach."

"Sounds perfect."

"We'll need to take my bike again." He's looking at me as if he's not quite sure what I'm into yet, which means I haven't quite made myself obvious enough. I would spend the rest of this week on the back of that bike if I could.

"I think I can live with that," I answer with a laugh, which makes him smile.

It doesn't take long to get to the food truck. It's parked with a few others at the locals' end of the island. Much like yesterday, it's so much quieter than the busier end. Locals are hanging out around the food trucks which are parked in a school's parking lot. They've all brought out their own camping chairs and beers.

They don't give me dirty looks or give me trouble for being with Logan. In fact, many of them greet him as he walks up. I would so much rather live in a community like this than the one my parents raised me in, where everyone is nice to you to your face and says terrible things about you when you're not there.

He buys an assortment of street tacos and has the cook put them in a plastic bag with a bunch of napkins. After a quick stop at the sleepy gas station on the corner for a six-pack of cheap beer, we're parked back at the same quiet cul-de-sac as last night. I can't help but notice that Logan is looking around the area like he lost something here.

"Everything okay?"

"Yeah," he answers, but it's not convincing. "Let's go."

We sit on the beach with the styrofoam boxes between us, devouring the tacos, which are spicy and full of flavor. My beer is going down way too fast. I think it's my nerves, being out with him by ourselves again, knowing that we are so close to something that excites me in a way I've never felt before. But after about fifteen minutes of small talk, I can feel my inhibitions fade away, and I want to say and do everything on my mind.

After the food is gone, we lean back and crack open our second beers. I'm still such a lightweight, so I know this second one will really push me over the edge, nudging me past that fine line between sober and drunk.

He's leaning back on his elbows, watching the waves as they roll and crash onto the beach. I'm sitting cross-legged next to him, wondering when he will kiss me and how far I'm willing to go if he does. A little part of me is screaming "all the way" while another, more cautious and conservative voice is hoping I'll be able to put on the brakes at first base.

Time seems to fade away without any progress. He

doesn't say much, just watches the water, looking at me from time to time to give me a small smile.

Maybe I didn't make it clear how attracted to him I am. The warm watercolor tattoos all over his arms are begging to be touched, and after half of my second beer, there is literally nothing between me and what I'm about to do.

I lean toward him, brush my fingers over his bare arms, and lean my mouth next to his ear. "Logan," I whisper.

His jaw tenses, his muscles flexing as he waits for my next words. His eyes stay trained on the water.

"I want you to kiss me," I say as I let my hand drift from his arm to his chest, then his stomach. Beneath my hands, I feel the growl rumble in his chest.

"You've had too much to drink," he says as he sits up and my hand drifts from his body to the sand. "You don't want that."

I let out a loud exhale. "Yes, I do."

"I should get you home. It's getting late." He shifts like he's about to stand, and I move with desperation. I grab his face and pull his lips against mine. His body is tense against mine, and after a moment, I pull my lips away, but he keeps his lips within an inch. Whatever his struggle is, I want to break away the barrier keeping him from me.

"You don't want me?" I breathe.

"Of course I do," he answers as his hand snakes around my waist and pulls my body closer. I can feel the crack in the barrier. I can see the light seeping through.

So I lean my body against his, my breasts against his chest as we're about to topple together into the sand. I push my lips toward his ear as I grab his hand and pull it toward my stomach as I whisper, "Please, Logan."

And it's just enough to break his resistance. He presses my body against the sand, letting his lips explore mine. His movements are all gentle and soft as his lips move along my jaw, back to my ear, and down my neck.

I let out a gasp as his hand moves to my thigh and under my dress to squeeze the flesh of my ass in his firm grasp. I feel as if I'm drowning in his touch, and I don't want him to stop. Every time his crawling touch stops, I feel my heart beg for more.

There's a hunger inside of me that is unleashed, and I wish so badly that he would kiss me harder and be a little more rough. It's as if I can feel his restraint. Like he thinks he can break me if he's too wild. And the wild is all I want.

I press my hips up to him, and the hardness beneath his jeans presses up against that spot between my legs. It's too much to bear. My hand shakes as I think about ripping the fabric between us away. Am I ready for that? The way he's making me feel right now, I am.

The hand that's not currently on my ass finds its way to my breast, pushing my cleavage into his mouth and without thinking of what I'm doing, I pull the strap off of my shoulder, letting my dress fall away to expose my entire breast.

Something about this makes Logan lose control as he digs his hips against mine and pulls my nipple into his mouth. My head falls back as the pleasure of his warm tongue against my skin makes something in my body come alive. What was once warmth in the pit of my stomach becomes a scorching heat that is searching, begging for release.

"Logan," I breathe as I wrap my leg around his body trying to pull him closer. There is no questioning voice in my head anymore. I want him inside of me with nothing between our flesh. Just his body in mine until we are one.

Suddenly, without warning, the warmth of his mouth against my skin is gone. The hungry pressure of his body against mine is gone. He pulls away and looks down at me with his eyebrows pressed down over his eyes and his mouth shut tightly.

"This isn't right," he says as he climbs away from me and starts walking away and shaking out his hands as if he's trying to shake off a feeling.

"What are you talking about?" I ask, breathless. The absence of his body against mine is devastating, and I would do anything to get it back. "I thought that felt incredibly right."

"You don't want to do this with me, Sierra."

"Yes, I do," I say as I stand and try to approach him, but he's keeping himself away from me like a scared animal.

"Let's get back. You should get home." He starts to walk back to the spot where he parked his bike.

I'm standing dumbfounded as he walks away. The buzz under my skin is gone, and now I just feel cold. Desperation is replaced with frustration and adoration is replaced with anger. I march after him and find him getting on his bike ready to start the engine.

"I honestly don't understand, Logan. What did I do wrong?"

"You're confused, Sierra. You don't want someone like me."

"I know exactly what I want."

"Get on the bike so I can take you home."

"No." I'm nearly shouting as I stand in my soft blue dress, yelling at this tattooed man on a motorcycle as if I'm the intimidating one. "I want answers. Is there someone else? Do you just not want me? Tell me you're not interested in me, and I'll go. But I know that's not it. I can tell you're keeping something from me."

"You don't know anything about me, Sierra. We don't know anything about each other, so yes, I'm keeping things from you, although I don't think any of them would surprise you."

"Try me."

"Fine. I'm an addict. Did you know that? Or that I'm a dealer. How does that sound to you? I've been in jail too. Still want to let me paw all over your body?"

Heat floods my cheeks, not because of what he is

confessing, but because he's finally opening up to me, letting himself be vulnerable for me. The truth floats between us, waiting for me to react.

Of course, I suspected these things. I've been watching Logan every spring and summer for years. I've seen his transformation, the darkness bleed into his eyes, and I hoped he wasn't struggling with addiction. I wanted him all to myself, not share him with that sinister illness.

"I don't care," I answer.

"You should."

"I can't explain the way I feel about you, but I'm drawn to you, Logan. I know that you're struggling. I know that you've had a rough past, but it doesn't change this attraction."

He looks up at me, his face stern and his chest heaving. I take my chance to move in, a little closer until I'm standing next to him. My hand reaches out and glides across his chest and around to his back until he pulls me close for a tight hug.

"I'm afraid you'll regret being with me," he says, his voice thick and smooth against my head.

"I'd regret it more if I passed on the chance to be with you." Then, I look up into his eyes, and he leans down until our lips are touching again. My body floods with heat as his hand cups my chin and his tongue glides across my lips.

He pulls away and lets our foreheads rest together. "Just this week, Sierra. This could never be anything more. Could you live with that?"

"Why?" I beg, wanting to kiss him again.

"Because you and I are from different worlds, and I'd rather have one week with you than let you ruin your life to be with me."

I disagree with every fiber of my being, but he seems so sure. If I can get a week, I'll take it. Plus, there's a part of me that is sure I could convince him to change his mind later.

"Deal," I say, balling his T-shirt in my fists and trying to pull him closer.

His lips find my neck again as he whispers, "I don't want people seeing you with me. If anything bad happens to me, I don't want you to get involved. Understand?"

"What—"

"Don't ask questions. Just tell me you understand."

"I understand," I breathe.

"And one last thing," he says, keeping just inches between us but driving me wild with the distance.

"Yes," I say, pressing my sex against his leg, needing more.

"No sex," he says, and the ache grows hotter.

"What. Why?" I beg, trying to kiss him as he pulls away.

"I don't want you to regret this week with me. I want to keep it pure."

"We won't make it," I tease.

"You have no idea what I'm capable of. Tell me you

agree."

I let my head hang back and let out a moan. This one feels too hard to agree to. My body is singing with desire, and the thought of never fulfilling that desire is a crippling prospect.

"Okay," I say as I look into his eyes.

"Good." With one hand creeping back to my ass again, he lifts my body so that I'm straddling the bike with him, facing each other. His mouth is on mine, no longer gentle and soft, but hungry and rough as he pulls my lips into his mouth with a bite.

He drags me closer until my legs wrap around his body. His kisses are giving me life. A warm hand reaches under my dress and climbs up to massage my breast making my sex pulse with heat. The other hand squeezes the back of my thigh again, pulling me so close that the few pieces of fabric between us is torture.

I stare into his eyes under the streetlights, so exposed and available for everyone to see, but I don't care. The street is so quiet and not one car has driven past while we've been out here. Plus, the thought that someone will see us only thrills me more.

I can't get enough of the way he growls into our kiss or the way he grinds the hardness in his pants against my core.

All too soon, he stops again. My chest is moving up and down with every heavy breath. Mumbling into my chest, he says, "Yeah, we're never going to make it if we keep doing this."

I can't help but laugh, and he leans up from my breasts to place a closed-mouth kiss against my lips.

"Come on," he says. "Let's save some for tomorrow."

"No," I moan against his mouth.

Then he lifts me off of the bike as if I weigh nothing at all. I climb on behind him, letting my fingers rest beneath his T-shirt and against his tight abs. My face rests against his back, and I breathe in the warm cotton smell of his shirt and the cologne beneath.

The drive home does nothing to cool the temperature inside of me. In fact, the vibration of the engine between my legs only makes the buzzing more intense. When we reach my condo, I climb off and kiss him again.

"You were unexpected," he says as I pull away.

I smile at him as I walk away. "See you tomorrow," I say as I climb the stairs toward my building. When I leave him, he has a gentle smile on his face. Not a look of happiness, but a look of peace and contentment. The most content I've seen him look since I met him.

I don't know how he can be so content, because I am on fire, and I'm afraid of what I've just gotten myself into.

Chapter Eight

LOGAN

They say the first three days are the easiest. But once you get to the third day, the addiction really lays its claws in and makes its last major pull. I wake up in a cold sweat and want to puke up everything. I wasn't a heavy user, but the little bit that I did have in my system is calling my name as if it's begging for attention.

Standing in the hot shower, I try to focus my mind on the feel of Sierra rubbing herself against my body. Her soft breasts in my hands and the sweet taste of her lips.

A wave of regret pours over me. I shouldn't have

done that to her. If she knew the filthy thoughts that went through my mind... I imagine her sitting at her house with dirt stains smudged against her white, clean dress. Does she regret it too?

I have to be at the shop at ten, but I get there at nine because I'm too restless to stay at home. We have a new shipment of supplies waiting to be unpacked and put away, so I get to work doing that, but it doesn't take long so I'm done by 9:15, feeling more restless than ever.

I could text her. Her number is in my phone waiting for me to act, to engage with her to ease the pulse of tension in my spine. Thinking about her has me confused about whether I'm jonesing for a hit or if I'm jonesing for her. Either way, I'm in ecstasy.

By the time Murph comes in, I have the entire shop wiped down and sparkling. He seems impressed until he puts two and two together. "What's up with you?" he asks through a side glance, his brows squeezed together and his thick, wide shoulders raised in question.

It takes me a minute to respond. I don't want to declare my sobriety too soon. If I fail, it's just another opportunity to let someone down. I don't want to say it yet.

"I got that girl in my head," I answer. He remembers Sierra from last night. He saw the way she lingered around me while I worked and how she couldn't sit still with me around.

"Good," he replies. "You need that girl in your life."

"What's that supposed to mean?" I'm not trying to be rude, but I can't shake the feeling that Sierra deserves so much more than me, and I'm not trying to use her to better myself.

"I mean that she's good for you. That you need someone nice in your life."

"You're nice," I joke.

"I'm serious, Logan. You don't need to be alone all the time."

"She's a spring breaker, Murph. She'll be gone in a few days."

He glares at me with his eyebrows raised and his head tipped in my direction as if he knows something I don't. So I wait for him to continue. "Logan. From the way that girl was looking at you yesterday, someone will have to drag her out of Wicked by her feet."

"That doesn't change anything. She's just another rich girl who wants a romp with a freaky local."

He stops what he's doing and turns toward me. "Look me in the eye and tell me that with a straight face."

I turn toward him, but my shoulders lack the confidence to repeat it. So I shrug and say, "I don't want to get attached."

To that, he just shakes his head and continues what he's doing.

The day passes like any other. There's a couple of morning appointments before we order lunch to be delivered. We sit in the back and scarf down our sandwiches as we both scroll through our phones.

Finally, out of nowhere, Murph bursts out, "Holy shit."

"What's up?" I ask, my mouth full of Italian spicy sub.

"Just got this text from Rafe. Some dude overdosed on the beach last night."

"Seriously?" Not extremely surprised, I don't really look up from my phone while I'm chewing. Rafe never texts me with his insider scoop from the station, but Murph is always quick to fill me in. Most of the time, I think he texts him just to make sure the dead body doesn't belong to me. This is how they fulfill their promise to my brother to watch over me.

Of course, Rafe never comes around or calls anymore, at all, and as one of my brother's oldest and closest friends, that puts a real damper on my perception of him.

"You know this kid?" He turns his phone to face me. The face peering back makes my blood go cold. Tyler is staring back at me, and even though I only met him the one time, and it was dark, I recognize his features immediately. His dark eyes, sharp cheekbones, and bright smile.

This isn't good.

"That's the kid who OD'd?" Taking his phone, I peer down at the face, waiting for this news to change somehow, but it doesn't.

"Yeah, do you know him?"

"Sorta."

Then Murph grows quiet as he stares at me. I'm still holding his phone, but I can feel the weight of his eyes. "Logan," he calls.

I don't answer, but he knows I'm listening.

"Did you deal to this kid?"

Looking up, I match his stare with the same intensity. "No. My stash was stolen."

"What are you talking about?"

I didn't mean to spill all of the details, but this new discovery has me leaking all kinds of information.

"I was supposed to deal Saturday night, but I got into a fight with this kid, and I left the party. That night my stash was stolen from my bike. That's what Hale's all pissed about."

"Jesus." His head falls back as he says it, and I know it's not a good sign. I knew I was in deep shit before, but now it feels like the water is rising around me.

"This can't be pinned on me. I didn't deal shit."

"But there are witnesses that can point you out, Logan. You were in a fight with this kid. They will remember you."

"Fuck." My face falls into my hands.

"Lost or not, those drugs are going to get back to you."

"Don't say that."

The front bells ring as we both curse in mumbles, wrapping up our lunches. Murph makes it out front before I do, so I take a few moments while he talks with the customer. The anxiety of this news about Tyler makes my cravings even worse. For now, I settle on a cigarette, even though I'd love to quit that too. I don't want to taste like an ashtray when Sierra finally comes to the shop.

SIERRA

"I think we can get these books to the front shelf if we get rid of those old magazines." I drop the box on the old chair as the old woman dusts off the nearly empty shelf by the front of the shop.

"People don't read magazines anymore, do they?" she asks as she pulls the dusty old magazines from the shelf.

They don't buy new magazines, let alone old issues that no one cares about anymore, but I don't say that to her as I start setting the new releases on the shelves. "Afraid not."

The shop is starting to look so much better already. We had three people walk in today to browse, and Mrs. Walker said that was more than usual by a long shot. We cleaned the front glass, put in some cute advertisements and arranged the display case to draw in customers. Now, my goal is to rearrange the inside of the store to get the people who come in to actually buy something.

She was so far behind in her inventory that the new releases from two years ago were still in the 'New Release' section which was poorly placed at the back of the store. Now we have it in the front, and I encouraged Mrs. Walker to create a 'Young Adult' section to appeal to the college crowd, as well as the moms who need an escape from their needy kids on their vacation.

She's been very accepting of the changes so far. I keep expecting her to kick me out and tell me to mind my own business, but instead, she just keeps asking me to stay forever and run the store for her. And all I keep thinking is that the invitation is very tempting.

We quickly lose track of time and before I know it, it's past two. Mrs. Walker made me a sandwich for lunch, and promptly ordered me to get out and go enjoy the sun for the rest of the day. Before I leave, I turn and marvel at the difference we made already. It's starting to resemble a cozy, inviting bookstore instead of a dusty old attic full of books.

There's only one place on my mind as I walk out the front door. The tattoo shop is just two doors up, so I slowly approach the window, hoping to get a glimpse of him working without him seeing me.

I'm in luck. Just as I reach the glass, I can see him. He's facing the window, bent over working on a back tattoo like it's an easel and he's a painter. His face is blank, but his stare is intense. With a slight squint to his eyes, he watches his own hands at work on the skin. The guy that he's tattooing is sitting backward on a chair, almost like a dentist's chair. It's reclined enough to make him comfortable, and rather than wearing a look of pain, he seems relaxed.

People pass me as I watch. He must be almost done because he pulls back and stares at the work, wiping a couple of times with a white towel. When the client says something, Logan laughs, the corners of his mouth lifting toward his eyes, creating delicate wrinkles at the edges.

I've never been more attracted to someone.

Suddenly, Logan sits back and sees me standing outside watching him like he's putting on a show. Smiling with a hint of embarrassment, I wave to him. He smiles a little more, and I can tell there is a blush there.

I walk in and lean on the glass counter as he finishes his work. He only needs to touch up the fresh ink because after a few moments, the client stands up to see the tattoo in the mirror, and my breath is lost. It is amazing. A cloud burst of color on his back, there is a gorgeous sunset that seems to be rising out of a skull. The bottom is dark, but the top is like an explosion of light and color. My hand covers my mouth as I watch him wrap it in plastic wrap and tape the sides with medical tape. He rings the customer up at the register and gives him his care instructions and ointment. As I watch him work, he sends me a subtle wink or acknowledgement every few minutes, and it sends butterflies through my stomach as he does.

The customer is a young guy I don't recognize. He thanks Logan and gives me a cordial greeting just before he leaves. Logan is still standing behind the counter. He rests his hands against the glass and gives me a quizzical look that screams of mischief.

"Are we alone?" I ask, peering around the shop. Aside from the heavy music playing through the speakers, the shop is silent.

"Sure are." He hooks a finger in my direction and summons me forward.

I play coy as I walk slowly toward the end of the counter. "I can't come back there," I say, giving him a playful smile.

"You can do whatever you want." He dares me to inch forward so I step behind the counter and within seconds, I'm standing against his body.

Long, torturous seconds pass by before he finally bends closer to press his lips against mine. The sweet spearmint taste of his lips sends chills down my spine, so when his lips brush between my own, I open them to let him in. His tongue brushes against mine, and there is an explosion of heat between my legs.

His kisses are so tender, yet intense. I feel so small in Logan's arms, and yet, he's so gentle with me that I feel entirely safe. He takes a nibble on my lip, and I respond by gripping his neck even tighter.

A low growl escapes his mouth as he pushes me against the counter, deepening our kiss. His hands slowly creep up under my shirt, tickling my sides and creating intense goosebumps across my skin.

All too soon, he pulls away and takes a breath. "What are you doing to me?"

I'm afraid he's going to stop, but he leans in and places a kiss against my neck. I try to hold him there, pressing my hips against his as a shameless tease. He counters by grinding into me with far more power, and I feel my eyes roll back in my head when his thick hardness presses into my lower belly.

I love that I do that to him. I've never been so intimate with a guy before, but I have a feeling that even if I had, I wouldn't get as high on his arousal as I do on Logan's. It makes me want him and not just physically. It makes me want to be the only girl who can do that to him. Forever.

"We can't do this here," he whispers into my neck.

"Then, let's go in the back."

A rumble of deep laughter vibrates against my collarbone. "You're a bad influence."

I laugh back, but I don't say that I wasn't kidding. I want nothing more than to go in the back of this tattoo shop and see how far we can take this.

Without warning, he hooks a hand under my backside and lifts me until I'm sitting on the countertop. Then he steps forward so his broad hips are between my knees. I'm not in a skirt today, which is regrettable since I almost always have a dress on. That easy access sure would have come in handy today.

Instead of touching me, he presses his palms flat against the glass. "You know, you are nothing like what I expected." He stares directly into my eyes, his crystal blues staring into my soul.

I curl my legs around his body and try to pull him closer as I smile. "What is that supposed to mean?"

"It means that you don't fit the stereotype."

"What stereotype?" I ask in a high-pitched voice.

"Oh, you know. Young, blonde, innocent..." His fingers drift slowly up my right leg, just past my knee, and stop before they reach the hem of my shorts. I squirm against the touch, wishing they would go further.

His hands leave my skin and go back to their spot on the glass counter.

"Well, you don't fit your stereotype either." My fingers find their way into his hair as I muss up the long, dark brown strands.

"How's that?" He leans his head back as I let my lips find his.

When I pull back after a short kiss with just a touch of tongue, I answer. "You act like such a big tough guy, but I know you're just a big softie."

He pulls away and stares at me incredulously, but in a way that makes me laugh.

"I can be a softie, but you know..." His hands find my hips as he jerks me forward, slamming his hips against my core, sending a thrill of heat up my spine. Then, into my ear he whispers, "I'm harder than you think."

I break out into flirtatious giggles as he nips at my chin. A door in the back opens and we pull apart in a rush as his co-worker rounds the corner into the front of the shop. He stops as he sees us and raises an eyebrow in our direction. I hop down and smile at him.

"Well, hello there."

"Hi," I murmur with a shy wave.

"You can go on your break," he says to Logan as he drops his bag by the chair farther back in the shop. My heart picks up speed as I turn toward Logan. The thought of having him to myself for a whole hour has my insides doing flips.

Chapter Nine

LOGAN

Sierra's walking so close to me, I can smell the flowery scent of her shampoo. She's in those short cut-off shorts, and they're driving me wild. As we approach the food trucks parked by the pier, I pull out my wallet to get her some food.

"I already ate lunch," she says.

"You look like you could eat again."

"I won't turn down gelato." She points toward the pink bubblegum covered van selling scoops of colorful ice cream to a line full of college kids.

We stand in line, and she keeps her arms around

my waist. It's like she can't help but touch me, and it's amazing, but it's also pure torture. I can't put my hands on her the way she touches me, not in public. Because once I start touching her, I won't stop.

No girl has ever had the effect on me that Sierra does. I've been with flirtatious girls and eager girls, but I never felt like it was really me they wanted. Just a warm body to fill some void.

"Why aren't you ever with your family?" I ask. It comes out a little ruder than I mean it to.

"They only bring me here so they can hang out with their friends. Golfing and tennis and God knows what else." She rolls her eyes. "They think I want to run around with all of these college kids, so they don't bat an eye at my being out all day and night."

"That doesn't seem right."

"They're a little older than most parents, and I'm an only child. So, they're pretty much over the parenting thing. They just want to live their own lives."

I can't hide the discontent on my face. I don't care what their excuse is. It's pretty lame to abandon your kid for a full week, especially on a beach full of drinking, sex, and drugs. Even if she is an adult now. They should want to hang out with her. I would.

When we reach the truck to put in our order, she orders a scoop of pistachio and insists that I get something. I don't have the heart to tell her that walking around the beach licking a scoop of ice cream on a cone is a real detriment to my image. She only smiles

SARA CATE

at me, holding back a laugh as the lady hands me a small bowl with a tiny purple spoon. I roll my eyes, which makes Sierra giggle even more into my shoulder.

"That's all you're eating?" she asks.

"I'm not hungry." Can't tell her why, though. Can't tell her that my stomach will barely be able to handle this little bit of sugar because it's doing flips in my gut right now, wishing it could just climb its way out of my body. The shake in my hands is gone and most of the urge is too, but the other side effects are still there. I may not have been a heavy user, but my withdrawal symptoms are a reminder that I was more addicted than I let myself believe.

"I have so many questions about you," she says as we walk down the beach sidewalk, the narrow planked walkway where the concrete meets the sand.

"You'll be disappointed by how much mystery I lack. What you see is what you get."

"I highly doubt that." She gives me a side glance as she licks the green gelato from the cone.

"What about you? There are so many things I don't know about you."

"Fire away," she answers with a smile.

"Why didn't you go to college?" I start.

"I didn't want to. I know that sounds like a rich brat kind of thing to say, but my parents wanted to spend a ridiculous amount of money to send me, and I just wasn't ready for it. I knew what I would find there,

·96·

and I wasn't interested. So I decided to take a year off...to think about my future."

"Did you figure anything out yet?"

"I figured out that I like the beach." Her body turns toward me as she walks and her left hand loops through my arm as she says, "Especially this one."

When I glance at her, I notice the way the brightness in her smile fades as if she's thinking about something that turns her mood. Perhaps it's the thought of ending up with a loser for a boyfriend who will only cause her pain and trouble if she chooses to stay with him.

"What about you?" she asks. "Why haven't you left Wickett?"

"My brother and I were raised on the mainland in the foster system, but my brother aged out before I did, so once I turned seventeen, I just ditched the family scene to live with him. He taught me everything he knew."

"He was a tattoo artist too?" she asks.

"No. He helped Murph run the business. He ran a lot of the business in town, actually. After getting his business degree online, he actually turned out pretty successful."

"Do you want to talk about what happened to him?"

There isn't a single part of me that wants to talk about what happened to Theo. The memory is a sour one, and the wound there is far from healed. But the way Sierra looks at me, like she's actually eager and open to letting me talk about my life, even the rotten bits, has me wanting to hold her.

We reach a small street when we stop, no longer surrounded by other beachgoers. So we take a turn and walk down between two buildings. It's quiet, secluded, but not as seedy as the alleyways by the tattoo shop. Once we find ourselves alone, she stops me and pulls my hand into hers.

"You don't have to if you don't want to," she says as she squeezes my fingers.

"I will at some point."

"That's okay, Logan." Her other hand snakes its way around my waist until our bodies are pressed together. And the contact lights a match inside of me, so I pull her closer and take her mouth with mine.

She exhales with a soft moan when I push her gently against the wall. The buzzing that has been ringing in my body all day, whether it be from her or my withdrawals, has finally found somewhere to release its tension so I deepen our kiss, pinning her body against the cool surface.

My mind is laser focused on one goal. I want to bring her pleasure, like it's some sort of misplaced craving. If I can't get high, then I want her to feel that ecstasy for me.

When my mouth leaves hers to travel down her cheek to her neck, she lets out a gasp. The sound sends a jolt of electricity through me, making me even harder. And the hunger becomes something far stronger.

My fingers search her body for something to make

her gasp like that again. Squeezing the flesh of her hips as I grind into her has her humming into my ear, but it isn't enough, so they travel farther down. First they find their way over her shorts until I'm rubbing her at the core and she begins to squirm against my hand.

Her lips are against my ear, her arms squeezing tight around my neck. I can't stop the growl that emits as I flip open the button of her shorts. They hang loose from her narrow hips leaving plenty of room for my hand as I let my fingers crawl down, under the light band of her underwear and over the short tuft of soft hair. Then, I feel her under my skin.

She's wet with desire, and I take a breath to appreciate how this beautiful girl is aroused by me. I let my fingers slide over the folds. Then, before entering her, I find that small spot of pleasure and I circle it, adding pressure with every round.

Panting now, her leg lifts until it's curled around my thigh, but it's still not the gasping sound I'm after. So, I let my finger tease the crease of her wet lips again before I finally plunge my finger deep inside of her.

Everything in her body tenses against me, and she lets out a loud gasp that echoes against the walls around us. Her head hangs back, and I push myself in again.

"Logan," she whispers, high-pitched and pleading. I move with the rhythm of her body as she grinds herself against my hand. I ignore the ache in my own pants as I push her closer and closer toward climax.

When her hand lets go of my neck, it's on the erection trying to bust out of my jeans, and I suck in a gasp from the pressure. I want to push it away because I'm too close to coming as it is. The tightness squeezing around my fingers as I dive into her again and again has me close to the edge.

"Logan, I'm almost there," she gasps as she squeezes the hardness through my pants.

I nip at the delicate skin of her neck. She's panting louder, letting out the sweetest moans, and I know I have her close. I'm getting high on her pleasure.

Then, just when I'm ready to feel her cum on my hand, I pull my finger back and direct the attention back on that sensitive little spot, and she squeals into my chest as her body freezes up in my arms. She's completely rigid through her orgasm, her legs squeezing around my hand still buried down her shorts.

She's hanging on to me as she shivers through the aftershock, still panting, and I know before she looks up at me that her cheeks will be red, but she won't be shy about it. I slowly pull my arm out of her shorts and she lets her weight fall back to her heels as her body relaxes against the wall behind her.

"Wow..." she sighs.

I can't hide the smile that seeps across my face. Red with pleasure, she has never looked more beautiful. As she stares up at me, she doesn't shy away from her sexuality, and I love her for that.

Her hand finds its way back to the front of my jeans.

"What about you?" she says, with a flirtatious smile on her face.

"You are a bad influence, you know that?" Leaning my hands against the wall behind her, I lean down to kiss her, softer this time. It's not a rushed kiss, but soft, warm contact with her tongue against my lips. I never want to leave this kiss. And even though I only made her come without my own release, I feel as if I'm coming down from the world's greatest high.

SIERRA

Something about Logan sets my body on fire. Those piercing blue eyes and those broad shoulders and just the right amount of muscle peeking through his tight-fitting shirts, but that's not what has me on edge.

It's the softness behind the tough exterior. It's the way he looks at me, after only two days, with such trust and compassion. It's the way he puts my pleasure first. Any girl would be happy to do dirty deeds in quiet alleyways with Logan, but they would never see in him what I do.

And I already hate the thought of leaving.

We don't say much on our walk back to the shop. He's hiding a smile, but the tension in his lips creates the most adorable dimples in his cheeks, like he has a dirty little secret. And I'm flying too high to speak.

I've been kissed, and I've done some pretty innocent making out, with mostly over-the-clothes stuff, but I've definitely never done that. I didn't even know another person could evoke that response from my body, and I already want to do it again.

I'm clinging to his arm like I need it to walk, which I almost do. My legs buckle every time I think about his hand in my shorts and the way he knew exactly how to get me all the way there.

Blue and red flashing lights ahead draw my attention away as we both stop to watch the police cars line caution tape around the area underneath the pier.

"What's going on?" I ask.

"Ummm..." he mumbles, and before he can answer, I see a few familiar faces in the small crowd that's starting to gather. Natalie's face turns back toward where I'm standing.

From this distance, I can tell she's crying. Her eyes are puffy and her face is contorted in anguish. "Oh my God..."

Stepping forward, I don't think as I cross the small street toward the beach. She makes her way toward me and begins to jog as we get closer to each other. Throwing her arms around me as we meet, she cries, "It's terrible! Oh my God, Sierra. It's so terrible."

"What the hell happened?"

As she pulls away, she wipes more tears from her face. Peering back at the crowd, I see her boyfriend walk toward us with a stern, tight expression on his face as if he's resisting the urge to show emotion.

"Fucking Tyler died last night," she says, her voice strangled and high-pitched.

The blood drains from my face as I stare at her, the words not quite registering as I look back toward the police tape. "What? How?"

"He got a bad batch. Someone killed him." Grant walks up behind Natalie and answers my question with a leveled tone, and he's not aiming it at me. His eyes are trained on someone behind my back. I turn around and see Logan still standing in the spot where I left him on the boardwalk. He's watching us with a guarded look on his face, eyes squinting and hands in his pockets.

"I don't understand..." I say, looking back toward Grant.

"Someone sold me drugs that were laced with something. And it killed him."

My mind is reeling as I stare at the two people in front of me. I didn't know Tyler did drugs, outside of the pot I could smell on him, but I guess spring breakers go all out when they have the opportunity. And to me, this sounds like a tragic mistake on Tyler's part, but the way Grant is glaring at Logan, I can tell they have other ideas about his death.

"I'm so sorry..." I touch Natalie's arm and turn to walk back to Logan when Grant's hand grips my arm, and his face gets only inches from mine. Out of instinct, I try to pull away, but he only squeezes tighter.

"Don't fuck around with that guy. He's nothing but a junkie. There's only one thing he wants from you, and if you give it to him, you'll regret it." My eyes go wide as he serves me a threat, disguised as a warning.

And just like I expected, Logan's voice is loud and thundering just behind me, his hand on my back. "You better fucking let her go."

Grant pulls away, his hand still on my arm like he's trying to drag me away with him. "Or what?"

"You wanna find out?"

"Stop it," I exhale, trying to wrench myself free from his powerful grip.

"There's a lot of cops over there. You really want their attention?" he threatens, while Logan's eyes drift toward the scene under the bridge.

"Grant, stop it." Natalie joins in my pleas.

"You think I'm afraid of going to jail?" Logan answers, standing a little taller.

Finally, after a long moment of tension between the two, Grant lets go of my arm, and I fall back toward Logan. I push him toward the street and back onto the path toward the tattoo shop, but he's heavy as stone.

"Come on, Logan. Let's go."

"Be careful with him, Sierra," Grant calls after us.

Finally, Logan relents and puts his arm around me as we walk back to where we were. My head is still reeling from this recent discovery. We walk silently again, but this time neither of us are hiding smiles. His arm is still around me as if he's protecting me, and I'm clinging to his arm, but my mind is going a mile a minute.

"I don't care about them. You know that, right?" Looking up at him as we come to a stop in front of his shop, I can see the way he averts my eyes and puts a wall up directly between us.

"That guy is an asshole. If he touches you again, I'm going to kill him."

"No, you're not." He turns away, and I put my hands on his chest to calm him. "Hey, look at me." Finally his eyes meet mine, but there's still too much anger there to see clearly. "I don't care about them. They have treated me like shit since I got here, and you've been nothing but amazing." My hands drift to his sides, feeling the tense muscles under his shirt. "I won't let them ruin our week."

His fingers grace my cheek and down to my chin as the fire in his eyes fades. Leaning down, he plants a soft kiss on my forehead, then my lips. His kiss is soft and gives me the feeling of comfort that I've been craving.

"What time do you get off?" I whisper against his lips.

"I'm on all night. You going to wait up for me?"

"Of course. I'll come back a little later..." I say in the form of a question.

He answers it with a pinch under my shorts that makes me squeal. Then, with a warm smile he smacks one more kiss on my cheek before I walk away and head home.

Chapter Ten

SIERRA

I can hear my parents talking when I approach the condo complex. It's only 2:00 p.m., and already it's been one of the most eventful days of my life. Even after learning about Tyler, my mind won't stop going back to those quiet moments together with Logan between the two shop buildings.

When I walk through the door, the hairs on my arm stand on end. I can hear the intensity in their voice. My mom is standing in the small kitchen talking with my dad who is sitting at the counter, reading something on his tablet.

"There she is," my dad mumbles as I walk in and

drop my keys on the table next to the door. The cross-body bag, with my sunscreen, phone, and other things, echoes through the condo as I drop it onto the floor.

"Sierra, sugar, did you know this boy?" My mom asks without looking up from the phone in her hands. I know who she's referring to as soon as she asks.

"I met him," I answer flatly without giving away anything else.

"Isn't this just terrible?" she shrieks.

"I sure hope you're not hanging out with the same crowd, Sierra," my dad says in a cold tone. He glances over his glasses in my direction.

"I'm not, Daddy. I met him at the bonfire on the first night. He was a little too wild for me."

"Well, I'll say so," Mom chirps as she puts down her phone. She walks up to me and gathers my hair in her hands and puts it behind my shoulders to look in my face. "Be careful out there, Sierra," she says.

"The locals are nothing but trouble," Dad adds.

"Tyler wasn't a local," I say, but they don't respond.

"They say the drugs were laced with something that killed that poor boy," he says without acknowledging me.

"Something the locals sell, for sure," Mom speaks to him.

"But he—" I try to talk, but they don't allow me one word. It doesn't matter anyway. They won't change their perception of the locals or of Tyler, no matter what I tell them.

My mother is still youthful and beautiful, only just turning forty-five last month. My dad is almost twenty years older than her, and it's without a doubt his money is what she married him for. Regardless, they've stuck together since before I was born and seem genuinely happy together. Happy...in that my dad still loves my mom's youth and beauty, and she still loves the luxury of his wealth.

I feel my mom's attention back on my face as she leans in and kisses my forehead. "Stay safe out there, sugar," she says just as she turns back toward the kitchen.

Before I know it, their attention is back on what's on their phones or each other. I'm just the tagalong again, so I escape to my room to hopefully grab a quick nap before going back out with Logan later tonight. Even if I have to hang out in the tattoo shop while he works, it will be more fun than hanging out here. Far more fun.

I sink down on the bed and grab my e-reader on the nightstand. We're only in the condo a few times a year, so the room is still pretty bare. After trying to read a few paragraphs, it's pretty clear that I won't be able to focus. My mind is going a mile a minute. I want to see him now. I want to feel the lust in his stare again. His hands on my skin. Down my shorts.

Nope. I can't do this here. I can still hear my parents talking down the hall. The condo isn't that big.

Instead, I lay back and think about the crystal blue

depth of his eyes, how it feels like I could swim there. Then, I remember my first spring break at Wickett when I first saw Logan.

My parents had just bought the condo, and I was only fourteen. I knew, even back then, that I wouldn't get along with the other kids that my parents' friends brought with them. Natalie was mean to me that first spring break because I was still fairly new and far less experienced than the rest of them. They were already exploring the bases when I had yet to even step on the field.

They had themselves convinced that because it was a small beach island, I couldn't get lost, kidnapped, or worse. So, just like this summer, I spent that one walking alone, eating alone, and sitting on the beach alone.

Then one day, I was sitting at the bookstore, reading through a pile of books that interested me when I saw him walk by. He was clearly older than me, maybe twenty, and I was instantly attracted to the fierce expression and mysterious demeanor. He walked next to an older man who was dressed nicely in a polo shirt and colorful pair of shorts. Logan was sporting his usual dark T-shirt and jeans.

They stopped in front of the window to talk, looking as if they were in a heated debate when Logan's glare turned on me. It was as if I caught his eye, and he couldn't look away. I was a scrawny middle schooler in a bookshop when everyone else was at the beach, and he was looking at me.

From then on, I couldn't get him out of my head. I found out that he worked at the tattoo shop as extra help in stocking and cleaning up, but since that wasn't an acceptable place for a young girl to hang around, I did a lot of walking, and every time I passed their storefront, I said a little prayer that he would be in sight through the window.

My heart skipped a beat every time I saw him. Through the years, I noticed that he began to collect tattoos, grew a little skinnier, and his eyes, although still blue, grew subtle dark circles under his lower lids.

For five years, I've watched him, loving him from a distance. Now that he's mine, I don't know how I'll be able to let him go.

LOGAN

I haven't stopped since getting back from lunch. I had one client after the next, mostly easy jobs and nothing too intricate. Butterflies, tribals, tramp stamps, oh my.

Murph is in a good mood tonight; the music in the shop is blaring, a few of his friends are hanging around the shop, and he even invited me to a party at his place after the shift ends, which he doesn't do often. Especially since Theo died, Murph hasn't been himself. No one has.

The close group of friends used to be inseparable, riding around town on their motorcycles and making oaths to always watch out for each other. Once they lost Theo, the group just dissolved without a word.

The parties used to be a Murph tradition, and it's how we knew he was on the uphill side of one of his moods. That man has the ability to flip a switch some days, so we take advantage of it when we can.

I respectfully decline the invitation, although I enjoy Murph's get-togethers. I make the excuse that Sierra will be with me, and I don't need her hanging out with that crowd. They're not really that bad, but they're on the older side, and mostly guys, so it can get rowdy. The talk gets foul, and everyone ends up drunk.

She shows up after nine, and I know it's her the second I hear the bells chime at the front. She's standing there with her hands behind her back in a little dress that stops above her knees. Instead of her squeaky clean Chucks, she has black Doc Martens, and the whole look is dick-hardening material.

"Holy smokes, you look great," I say in front of everyone, and she immediately blushes.

Even my client, a barely eighteen-year-old girl getting 'Princess' tattooed down her arm—fuck my life—looks up and admires Sierra's perfection. "Cute boots," she says before laying her head back down on her other arm.

Cute is not the word I would use. I don't know

what word I would use because my brain isn't getting enough blood to think of words right now, but cute is definitely not it.

"I'll just hang out here until you're off, if that's okay," she says as she sits down on the empty chair next to mine. We used to have three artists in the shop, but the other guy left a couple years ago, and Murph hasn't even looked for anyone new. He doesn't do too well with change.

"That's fine. It might be a while..." I warn her. "We have people waiting."

"No problem. I like hanging out here."

Murph rounds the corner, checking his most recent client out at the front register. He sees Sierra and stops to do a double take. "Hey, there! You look like you're ready for a party."

I glare up at him with a warning look. When his eyes lock on mine, he only laughs at the intensity of my expression.

"Just hanging out," Sierra answers him.

"Well, talk your boyfriend into bringing you to my party later. He should be showing you off." He gives her a wink, and I don't have to look up to see it.

"Murph." My curt warning does nothing as he walks off, laughing, his deep voice echoing through the shop.

I finish the princess tattoo, seal up the ink, and give her the instructions she needs. When I walk back to sanitize my station and get ready for my next customer, Sierra is watching me with a glare full of lust and temptation.

God, I want to wrap those boots around me.

"A party sounds fun," she says through her hooded lashes.

"No way."

"Why not? Afraid I'll find a moodier tattoo artist there?" She's leaning over the side of the chair with one of her legs tucked under her butt. It's doing two things. Pushing her tits up to her chin and nearly out of the top of her little dress. And hiking up the short length of her dress to reveal most of her thigh and a little of her ass.

I march over to her and lean down, placing my hands on either side of the chair. Then, with my face just inches from hers, I pull her dress down over her back-side and say, "No. I just want you all to myself."

Planting my mouth on hers, I deepen the kiss, teasing her tongue with my own. We have an audience, so I pull away before things get too steamy. As I turn away to call my next client with a smile on my face, I notice Sierra squirming in the seat, obviously panting and wanting more.

It's almost midnight by the time we close up and head out. Murph has his arm around Sierra as we walk down the street toward his place, which is only a few blocks from the shop.

I'm helpless against them now. He has fully convinced Sierra that the party needs more beautiful girls, and when she promises him that she doesn't have any eligible friends that he would want—even for the night—he convinces her that at least she has to show up. To pretty the place up.

I give him another look of death as she relents.

"Come on, just for an hour."

"I'm sure an hour can't hurt," she adds sweetly before looking back at me with an embarrassed grin. It's obvious she wants to go, so I don't even argue.

Murph's parties are always very low-key in that everyone brings their own beer, the music is Murph's choice, and everyone stays out back where the view is the best. For a beach island, he has the best yard in the whole town. Sitting a little higher than the rest of the island, he has a perfect view of the moon over the pier. The fact that he lives in such a nice house with a view and a huge garage to store his multiple bikes, Murph continues to be the biggest anomaly on the island. Even Theo couldn't figure him out.

There are already at least a dozen people there by the time we arrive. He lets people in before he gets there to let them set up and put the coolers out. The party will easily run until sunrise with as much beer as they bought, but it's tradition for Murph's parties anyway. A bunch of drunk nocturnal locals.

"I can see my parents' condo from here," Sierra whispers to me as we find an empty lawn chair, and I pull her onto my lap. I don't miss the way she calls it their condo and not hers, like she's a visitor or something.

"Which one is it?" I ask. She turns around to point to the tall white building with large balconies and a high-end style architecture.

"That one on the left. Third floor. If they look out their window, they might actually be able to see us."

"Well, then you should give them something to look at," I joke, and she turns to me with a lustful expression. She stands and turns to straddle my seat.

This girl is constantly challenging my preconceived notions about her. She is daring, wild, and stubborn. By the look in her eye, I can see the rebellion. And I know that I play that part for her. The wild rebellion in her normally squeaky clean life.

I am a check mark on her bucket list.

As her soft thighs squeeze my hips, I thank my lucky stars that she's checking the box on that list with me.

"Is this better?" she asks, looping her arms around my neck.

"I think so." She leans in and kisses me, a soft and wet kiss that turns me on as much as it gives me those warm and terrifying thoughts.

Thoughts like wanting to kiss her forever.

Thoughts that belong to other guys, the kind of guys who get down on one knee, build picket fences, and say those forbidden three words.

I growl against her kiss and pull her hips closer to my body. The cruel voice in the back of my head is a subtle reminder that we are here to be physical, have a little fling, and that is all.

"Get some, Logan," someone bellows from across the yard. I recognize the voice as Ezra's, another one of the guys who used to run in Murph and Theo's gang. Instead of returning with a roast, I just flip him my middle finger and let Sierra trail her kiss from my mouth to my neck.

"Leave them alone," Murph defends us. "They're young and in love." He's drunk already. I have my suspicions that he may have started a little early, not that you could tell with his work. Some people work a little better on the sauce. How that works, I have no idea.

But his sloppy talk has me tense and pulling away from Sierra's kiss. She giggles against my neck at Murph's words. I don't know if she's embarrassed or uncomfortable, but I don't want her feeling out of her element, although she totally is.

"Let's get out of here," I whisper.

"I like hanging out with your friends," she responds, which just makes me tense even more. Hanging out with friends is relationship zone stuff. "These aren't my friends," I say loud enough for them to hear.

"They're better than my friends," she echoes, and they all respond with encouragement.

"That is true," I say.

"I like her," Murph says as he leans forward to clink his bottle with hers. After the two cheer each other, she gets up from my lap and asks for the bathroom.

Murph gives her directions, and I can't help but gloat at him after she's gone.

"What the hell is wrong with you?" he says.

"I shouldn't have brought her here," I answer, taking a swig.

"Why? Because we're treating her like your girlfriend and not your booty call?"

"She's not a booty call," I say, feeling suddenly very defensive at the idea that that's how they see her. "We're not even having sex, not that it's any of your business."

"Well then, smile a little, Logan. She's great. Beautiful. Sweet. Good for you, man."

"She's here for a few days, Murph."

Then he stops arguing and just looks at me with a curt nod and a deep inhale. Like he suddenly understands. I like this girl. And the more I'm with her, the more I like her. So, what the hell is going to happen to me after this week is over?

Sierra was the life of the party for the rest of the night. It was easy to see how much the guys loved her. She kicked ass in beer pong, swearing she had never played in her life. Just after 3:00 a.m., I can tell she's yawning in secret.

I lean over to her and put my lips to her ear. "I'm ready when you are."

She glances up at me, eyes full of desire and warmth. "Okay."

Without another word, she starts making her rounds, saying goodbye to all of these rough-edged guys who had all fallen under her spell the moment she arrived.

We walk toward her condo slowly. I can feel her buzzing next to me, and the tension in the air screams of lust and expectation. How am I going to make it a whole week without devouring this girl whole? Even now, my body is throbbing with desire to just touch her. As if every moment that our skin isn't in contact is some sort of torture meant to destroy me.

All I want is for her to destroy me.

Finally, she loops her arm through mine. "I wish this week could last forever," she whispers as we approach the parking lot outside her building.

The word 'forever' hangs in the air between us, and I'm struck dumb without knowing how to respond to that. I can't give her forever. I can't even give her more than seven days.

As much as I want to. As much as that growing tenderness makes me want so much more, I have to constantly remind myself that she deserves far better.

And I will not let myself pretend that forever is an option.

So, I don't respond. I don't agree with her, and I can feel her slump when I stay silent. She stops our walking and turns toward me, wrapping her arms around my waist and pulling my body against hers.

Why does this precious thing even care about me? What could she possibly see in a loser like me? I'm too broken. Too rough and lost. When she could literally have anyone she wants, why would she even bother for a moment with me?

"I'm glad you're having fun," I whisper against the top of her head.

She pulls back in reaction and looks up at me with her eyebrows tight and confused. "You still think..."

She stops, then shakes her head as her eye contact floats to something other than my face.

I'm dying to know what she has to say, but I don't ask.

"Get some sleep," I say before I lean in to give her a chaste, quick kiss on the lips that she barely returns. Somberly, she pulls herself away and walks into her building.

On my walk back to the shop to get my bike, I start to notice that my hands aren't shaking anymore. Even after just two beers, I don't feel like puking my guts out and can actually focus on something other than my next—nonexistent—fix.

Sierra is my new drug. When she's around me, I don't care about smoking anything. Fuck, even the cigarettes I've cut way back on. She's like a fucking miracle cure. As if being around her fills the gaping holes in my life that I used to fill with something else.

Chapter Eleven

SIERRA

I can't stay away. I literally can't. When I wake up in the morning, the first thought that welcomes me every day is the vision of Logan's taut muscles across his chest and stomach, the feeling of his hand against my skin, and the exhilaration of having a full orgasm right in the middle of the day out in broad daylight by someone else's hand.

I have never felt more alive, and all I want to do is be around him with his bright smile. And although it's rare, that's what makes it so much more precious.

When he does smile, it's for me. Just me.

The feeling of overpowering ownership consumes me. I don't want to just enjoy my time with Logan. I want him to be mine. I want to call him mine. To know that I am the only girl on his mind, now and every day after.

I'm sitting in the shop the next day, reading a book behind the front desk because Murph says I'm drawing people in with my "wholesome hotness."

I couldn't help but giggle at Logan's growling reaction to that declaration. "She's not bait."

"No. She's good for business." Then he gives me one of his famous Murph winks before heading to the back to do inventory. That man is an enigma.

Smiling at Logan, he glances up and gives me a knowing look before he bends back over to finish the unicorn tattoo on this girl's ankle. Her friend glances back and forth between us. I can see the question in her eyes, wondering whether or not we are a real couple.

It's almost lunchtime, and even though I offer to do a food run, Murph cuts in and tells me to stay while he runs out. Just as he snakes out the back of the building, Logan finishes the unicorn, and I hover over to admire the beautiful work.

He is so talented. He has a way of making such simple drawings come to life with color. The girl gave him explicit instructions to make it as "colorful as fuck," in her exact words. And did he ever.

Even with the redness of her skin from the needle, the pink and purples in the unicorn's mane are practically moving with life. Her skin is radiating, and I can't help but feel a little jealous. And not just because he's had his hand all over her leg for the past two hours.

We both wave the pair off as they leave. Neither of us neglect to realize that we are now alone in the shop. I drop my book on the chair and give Logan my full attention.

Within a second, his hands are on my hips and he's pushing me against the wall. "There's another way we can draw attention." He growls against my neck as his fingers trace the edge of my skirt.

I love the feel of his body against mine. It truly makes me feel alive, like the heat that flushes through my core is what gives me life, a lustful breath of deliciousness.

"I like it," I giggle as his lips take mine, and we hum together, devouring each other like a meal we've been waiting for. And when he pins me tighter against the wall, I feel my legs part of their own accord to allow his broad hips room to fill the empty space.

"I have an idea," I whisper as his mouth leaves mine to roam over my neck and collarbone.

"That scares me," he says with a throaty laugh.

"I want a tattoo," I answer, looking over at the empty chairs on the other side of the room.

"No way." His response comes out in a deep tone

vibrating against my skin.

"Why not?" I pull back, but he latches back on like a magnet.

"Because tattoos are forever."

"Isn't that the point?" I gasp as his hand finds its way to the bottom hem of my skirt, lifting it enough to glide his hand up my thigh to squeeze the flesh.

"Stop trying to distract me," I breathe, but he doesn't listen. His hands roam their way along the edge of my panties until he's right back to where he was yesterday. Part of me wants to stop him, only because he's being far too generous, and it's starting to feel unfair. But the other part of me wants nothing to do with that plan because Logan's hands on my body is like a special kind of magic that makes every inch of me hum with pleasure.

My head falls back against the wall, my eyes falling closed as he plays my body like a musician plays his instrument.

But something makes me open my eyes. Maybe I hear the voices before I see the familiar faces walking down the sidewalk outside of the shop. And just as Logan's fingers are about to dip between the gentle folds, I let out a quick yelp and drop to my knees, hiding myself behind the counter.

Logan is left standing with his hands still in position but no longer holding the girl writhing with pleasure. His face follows me as I crouch, his eyebrows pressed together in confusion.

"Everything okay?" he asks.

Then, I hear the one sound I do not want to hear. The doorbell chimes as my parents' voices fill the room with their bland, leveled discussion, complaining about something to each other and taking a full ten seconds before they even acknowledge Logan, who is still standing dumbstruck with my pleasure on his hands.

"Can I help you?" he asks, looking cautiously up to the strange couple who just entered the shop.

I'm dying, curled up in an uncomfortable position behind the counter, leaning on Logan's leg for support. Did they find out that I'm here? Who would tell them? Or—oh God—are they here for tattoos? I'd literally die.

"Yes," my father says after clearing his throat. "We were told that Mr. Douglas works here."

"Murph is out to lunch," Logan answers without flinching.

I'm clinging to his tight jeans and when I glance up to see his face, I can't help but notice that the effects of our very recent contact is still there, proud and obvious.

Oh my.

I see him swallow as I stare up at him, a mischievous smile playing on my lips. The quickest of glances downward proves that he sees my face. And I swear, I literally can't help what I do next.

My hand silently and very languidly begins to travel

up his leg, murderously slow.

His leg jerks, like he's trying to shake off a pest.

But he keeps his eyes trained on the couple in the lobby.

"Well, we made a formal complaint to the housing authority about a loud party last night that we believe came from Mr. Douglas's house." My father's voice is rigid and drab, like he's so disappointed in Logan and he wants him to hear it. It's so annoying, and honestly, it eggs me on to keep having a little fun with Logan—at his expense.

"It was so late," my mother whines. "Must have been past 2:00 a.m."

Logan clears his throat as my hand moves from the inside of his thigh to the solid mass straining the front of his jeans. He tremors under my skin, and I have to suppress a laugh when I see the effect. It's just getting worse for him, which only makes me hungrier with power.

"Yeah, well—" Logan clears his throat. "I'll let Murph know you stopped by." Logan shakes his leg, trying to shake me off. I squeeze in response, rubbing my palm a little harder. He pins my hand between the backside of the counter and his body and grinds against it. I catch his eyes rolling in his head so subtly that even if my parents caught it, they'd probably just assume Logan's on drugs.

"Yes, please do," my mother says. Then, I hear the shuffling of her feet as she walks around the small lobby of the quaint tattoo parlor. I keep my breathing silent as I hear her loose bracelets hit the glass of the counter and know she must be peering down at the jewelry on display.

My hands freeze when the room grows silent.

"Anything I can help you with?" Logan asks, politely but with a hint of irritation in his voice.

"God, I hope Sierra doesn't get any of these piercings," she tells my father, ignoring Logan behind the counter. I can see his nostrils flare, biting down the urge to tell her off.

My dad scoffs. "Sierra wouldn't come to a place like this."

Logan clears his throat. I can see his eyes travel back down to where I'm hiding.

Which only makes me question why I'm hiding at all. Why don't I stand here with him, proud to be his friend, or whatever we are? But just as I'm about to stand and say fuck it all, I hear the bells chime as my parents leave.

The moment they're out of sight, I'm being lifted up like a ragdoll and pinned against the back wall while Logan attacks my mouth with this. He nibbles at my lips as he kisses me, grinding his erection against my core, and I love this undone version of him. I make a mental note to drive him crazy more often. The result is delicious.

"This week is going to kill me," he groans against my lips.

I wish I could help him find relief, but Murph will be back any second, and we don't have the time for anything else. Finally, he pulls away and paces around the room like an injured animal. Holding his hands on his head, he takes long, deep breaths.

"Sorry," I mumble.

"Don't be. You're more fun than I expected." He winks at me.

"They're awful. I'm sorry," I say, hoping to lighten the mood.

"Don't apologize for them. But why not just be honest with them? If you don't want to go to college, just tell them. You want to stay on Wickett, just tell them."

"It's not that easy, Logan."

He plants a quick kiss on my lips before walking away to clean his station and put away some supplies.

"This is all very Dirty Dancing," I say with a sly smile.

He stops working and glances back at me. "What the hell are you talking about?" he asks.

"Dirty Dancing. You know...the rich girl and the local boy with a bad reputation."

"You think I have a bad reputation?" He winks at me as he tosses a bottle of water from the mini fridge my way. I catch it and watch him.

"Wait. You've seen Dirty Dancing, right?"

"Can't say that I have," he says, and my jaw drops.

"Well I know what we're doing tonight."

"Watching a movie?"

I can see the hesitation in his expression.

"Yeah. We can watch it at your place."

"Uh..." he grumbles.

"What's wrong with that?" I ask, leaning against the counter.

He turns and walks toward me, placing both hands on either side of the counter, blocking me in. "Well, for one," he says, tilting his head, teasing me with the hope of a kiss that he pulls away. "I live in a small one-room studio apartment above the shop, so probably not what you're used to. And two," he continues, pulling back and leaving me breathless. "I'm not sure you and I could be alone together in my apartment if we want to keep up our bargain."

He presses his hips up against my body, and heat floods my veins again.

"Those were your conditions," I breathe.

His lips touch my neck, and I let out a moan involuntarily. He's driving me crazy on purpose. I reach for him to pull him closer, but he pulls away.

The back door opens, interrupting us as Murph stomps into the shop. Logan turns away and gives me a wink before greeting his boss. I'm left panting against the counter, wanting to murder and screw Logan all at the same time.

LOGAN

Business is slow, so Murph lets me leave a little early. One of his buddies came in to cover the desk, which is a pretty typical thing for him to do.

I push away the worrying reminder that I have business with Hale to tend to at some point, but for now I have to clean up for Sierra.

I've had girls in my apartment before, and I normally wouldn't give two shits about how it looks. They're usually not there for the ambiance.

But this is Sierra, and I care about the kind of environment she's in. Even having her at Murph's party had me on edge. She deserves the best, and I already hate the thought of her walking in, too distracted by the humbleness of it all to want to spend any time with me.

I'm actually a really tidy guy, considering. I'm constantly cleaning the shop, and I'm barely home enough to make much of a mess, so a once-a-month cleaning haul of the single room is enough to get the job done. I must have gotten it from my brother, or having lived my entire life in someone else's overrun and chaotic home. Finally, now that I have one of my own, I want to live in something as close to perfect as possible.

If only I treated my body the same way.

The irony is not lost on me.

So it really doesn't take me long to get the place ready.

Before she left the shop today, she said she'd come by around nine. I went to the market down the street to at least make sure I had food and drinks for her. I hope she doesn't mind cheap beer and snacks.

I don't even know how we're going to watch this, so I hope she brings something. I don't even own a TV. I must be nervous because I'm obsessing over everything.

It's not about being around Sierra; I've seen her so much this week that I feel strange when she's not around. It's the fact that we are going to be alone, in a confined space, with nothing but time and each other's bodies.

Damn, my dick is throbbing just thinking about it.

It's only 8:45, and already I'm pacing.

Thank fuck, the tap on the door echoes through the apartment just after I check the clock for the tenth time. When I open it, I'm instantly hit by the delicate scent of her perfume, or soap, or whatever it is.

She's standing there with her hair in a ponytail and a thick sweater over her shoulders covering her little dress that she had on earlier. She's carrying a beach tote with a bottle of wine sticking out and what looks like a tablet.

"This movie is downloaded and ready," she says with a smile before I let her in.

Her thin legs stick out of the bottom of her short dress, and I want nothing but to creep my hand up to see where they go. Movie be damned.

"Come on in," I say with a smile. She doesn't hesitate as she drops her bag by the door. I can't help but notice the way her eyes stay on me without doing that thing where people look around a room they enter for the first time, scoping the place out. She doesn't care about my apartment.

She loops her arms around my neck and presses up to kiss me, and I respond by tucking my hand under her ass and pulling her body against mine.

Our kiss gets heated as I press her against the back of the door after shutting it. There's no way I'm going to make it through a movie with this hard-on.

Hopping down from my hold, she mumbles against my ear, "Now, now. We have a deal and a movie to watch." Then she slithers out of my hold and walks toward the center of the room. I catch her standing in the middle of the room, looking around.

Oh shit. It's too small. Or just too fucking depressing.

Her hands rise in the air as if she's confused. "Where's your couch?"

"It's a studio," I laugh. "I don't have a couch."

"So we have to lay on your bed to watch the movie?" she says, glancing back at me with a mischievous grin.

"Yeah," I answer, rubbing the back of my neck. Fuck, I feel like a creep. This was a terrible idea.

Then she just climbs on my bed and sits against the headboard, patting the space next to her. "Fine by me. You're the one who's going to struggle."

I let out a laugh, watching her and all of her boldness. Her bare legs are crossed on my bed, and I think I might actually die from having to watch this movie next to her.

About twenty minutes into the movie, I find myself getting really interested in the story. So much so that I stop thinking about Sierra's legs draped over mine. Or the smell of her shampoo in my nose as she rests her head on my chest.

She's halfway through her bottle of wine so I slow down on my beer. I don't want to break our deal, and I especially don't want to be doing it because we're both drunk.

"This is the best part," she whispers. It's another dance, and I can see why she says that. Even I'm tapping my foot along with the music.

When the credits finally roll, it's almost midnight. Sierra stretches her legs next to me, and suddenly, the expectation in the air is almost suffocating. She glances up at me, and I notice her cheeks and ears are redder than normal, probably due to the wine.

Even after stretching, she doesn't get up from her place on the bed, half on top of me, and half next to me. Instead, she rolls onto her stomach next to me and reaches up to nuzzle her face into my neck.

Having her so close has my heart pumping in my chest. She has to be able to hear that.

"Easy," I mumble, even though I do not want her to

go easy. At all.

"Why?" she groans, drawing out the word.

"Because I trust you even less than I trust myself."

She pulls away and looks into my eyes. "Why don't you want me?" she asks, and my jaw drops. She catches herself and fixes her question. "What I mean is... why would it be so bad if we were together?"

"I don't want to be your first, Sierra," and she scoffs at me, which is adorable. Her perfect face with those angelic blue eyes hardly does her temper justice. She couldn't pull off grumpy if she tried. So, I tuck her hair behind her ears and explain myself. "That sort of thing stays with you forever. And you won't be around for more than a week. You should give that to someone who can give you a real future, Sierra. Someone worth it." Saying that out loud is nearly as painful as thinking about it. I never want another person to touch Sierra, but it's a far better scenario for her to have a better chance than to give herself away to someone like me.

She tilts her head to the side and watches me as if she's trying to figure me out.

"I don't understand why you don't see what I see, Logan."

"Because you don't know how low I've been."

Then she rests her head on my chest again, and I feel a powerful tug to hold her close. I want to wrap my arms around her, not just now, but for so much longer. And as much as I tell her that I want her to find someone worthy, I absolutely fucking hate the idea of another guy pawing all over her. What if he isn't gentle? What if he doesn't know how goddamn amazing and delicate this girl is? What if he takes her boldness as an invitation to be too rough or too demanding? My stomach turns at the idea.

If I thought it meant she would stay and that I could keep her safe, I would do it now. I would flip her over on this bed and make sure she came at least three times before I even thought about my own pleasure. I would ease into her so gently, keeping her safe from pain. Then I would own her tight little body all night long, making her completely mine, now and forever.

And when we came together, I would memorize the sound of her voice as she said my name.

But I know better.

I can feel her slender body moving against mine. She's restless. So when she sits up to kiss my mouth, I expect it. I bury my fingers in her blonde strands, pulling her lips impossibly close until we are breathing the same air.

When she pulls away, she doesn't go far. She throws her leg over my body so she is straddling me. Then she sits back, and I'm struck by her beauty. This fucking miracle sitting on top of me, her hair draped around her face like a veil, looking down at me with eyes full of lust.

When she grinds her body against my hips, rubbing herself against the hardness in my pants, I lose my breath.

"What are you doing to me?" I groan.

She leans down, her perfect hair gliding across my face. "I wish you would change your mind." Then, she reaches for the hem of her dress, and in one swift motion, she pulls the light fabric and her sweater up and off, leaving her half-naked and perched on my dick like a goddess.

"Sierra," I growl, but she has too much power over me now. My hands graze the soft skin of her hips as she lays her body flat against mine.

"You don't give me enough credit, Logan. It should be up to me who I spend my first time with, and to me, the only person who deserves it is you." Then her mouth is on mine, and I lose myself in her.

She's pulling my shirt up, and I let her. The feel of her bare stomach against mine is the sweetest thing I've ever felt.

I can't get enough of her, trailing my lips over her mouth, her chin, her neck, then her chest. I slip out one of her perfect little tits and let my tongue glide over her pink nipple. Her head falls back in pleasure.

It feels as if we're jumping off of a cliff together, so I wrap my arm around her hips, pressing her tighter and tighter against my body so that if we fall, at least we don't fall alone.

There is no stopping us now. I couldn't if I tried. All I see is Sierra. And all I want to see for the rest of my life is her in this very moment.

So, when she reaches for the button of my jeans and

moans for me to take them off, I obey. My hands fumble with the button while she continues to kiss my neck—

A loud banging on the door jolts us both. She gasps and moves to cover herself.

We both freeze for a moment, looking at the door. I pull her closer to protect her, though from what I'm not sure.

Quickly, I flip her off of my body while I jump up to put myself between her and whoever is at the door. "Stay back here," I bark. She grabs her dress from the bed and quickly throws it on without another word.

My first instinct is the police.

In the next thought, I'm sure it has to be Hale.

"Who is it?" As I approach the door, I stand away from the doorframe, just in case someone wants to ambush me as I open it.

"Murph. Open up." My shoulders relax as I look over to Sierra for the first time since the banging on the door pulled us apart. Before she lets herself relax, I catch a moment of that terrified expression on her face.

Which only makes me feel like a real dick. I can't stand the thought of her being so scared in my apartment. In my life.

She doesn't belong here.

I flip back the latch on the door and pull it open to reveal Murph standing there with a less than happy scowl on his face.

"Cops showed up at the shop," he murmurs, clearly keeping it quiet enough so Sierra can't hear. It doesn't do much good because when I look over at her, I can tell she heard. Her eyes are as wide as saucers.

It was fun while it lasted, I think. There's no way she's going to stick around now.

"Let me walk her home. Then you and I can talk, okay?"

Murph's hard expression changes from stern to something close to sorry.

"Make it quick," he bites out just before turning away and walking toward the staircase on the other end of the hall.

I send him a quick apology, but he only lifts a hand in response. He's pissed, and he never truly bothers to hide it. Can't say I blame him. If the cops showed up at my business looking for my junkie employee, I'd be seething too.

When I shut the door and turn toward Sierra, she's a few steps closer, almost within arm's reach. I'm going to miss kissing her, and it hits me like a ten-ton truck.

"Everything okay?" she asks, innocently.

I can't even answer, so I just shrug. "Let me walk you home."

"Logan," she says. Suddenly her hand is on my arm. "You didn't do anything wrong."

"It doesn't matter." I grab my shirt and throw it on before reaching for my shoes tucked neatly under the bed.

"It does matter. They think you sold Tyler something, don't they?"

"I wonder who gave them my name." My voice is laced with sarcasm, and I didn't mean for that to come out so cold. This has nothing to do with her.

"I was with you the night before Tyler died. I've been with you this whole week. I know you didn't do it."

"This isn't Dirty Dancing, Sierra." My tone is too harsh, but I just want her to leave. Not because I don't want her around, because I do. Having her in my apartment feels like someone opened a goddamn window to let the light in for the first time. I just don't like her in this situation. I don't want her mixed up with the cops, drugs, or me.

Look at me, starting to really care about this girl.

This whole week is fucked.

She's watching me with a stubborn look on her face. She's not going to give in that easily, I can tell.

After a quiet walk home, she leaves me with a long kiss, a kiss that feels like a promise. One I can't wholeheartedly return.

All I keep thinking as I walk back to the shop to talk to Murph is that if I get arrested for this, then I deserve it. Not because I sold anything bad to Tyler, but because I had intentions to sell at all.

In my mind, it's just as bad to almost sell a kid a shit-ton of drugs as it is to actually do it.

When I reach the shop, it's quiet, and Murph is

waiting in his office at the back. It's just a small storage room with a desk, but it has a chair big enough for Murph. He's leaning back with his arms crossed, waiting for me.

"Spill it," he bellows as I walk in. Murph has seen enough bullshit in his life to be able to see right through it.

"I didn't sell that kid shit." It feels good to speak the truth, even if I'm not entirely guiltless.

"Then why are the cops showing up at my shop?" he asks.

Any other boss would fire me. I'm too much trouble, even when I'm innocent. But Murph isn't any boss. He's my brother's best friend. And when my brother pulled Murph out of trouble, he promised to return the favor.

They had a pact. As close to family as any of them ever got.

"Because some punk kids thought it would be fun to give them my name."

"Are you using?"

"No," I answer as softly as I can. Again, it feels good to be honest. I haven't gotten high in four days.

"Are you selling?"

Here's where I hesitate. Murph notices because he leans forward and lets out a long exhale, balancing his elbows on his knees.

I pull up a black folding chair and straddle it backward, letting my head fall into my hands.

"I'm in debt."

"To that little fuck?" Murph bites out, referring to Hale. He knows it all without even having to ask.

I nod.

"So he's making you take the fall for him, Logan."

"I realize that."

"As long as he keeps you in the red, he controls you."

I nod along. I'm not one to be lectured, but Murph gets it. He says all the things I already know, but I let him chastise me because I fucking deserve it.

"I can't get out of the red this time," I say. Looping my fingers together, I press them against the back of my head and look up at the ceiling. This is the part that hurts.

"Why not?"

"Because I lost the stash I was supposed to sell." It comes out with an exhale, and Murph's eyes go wide as saucers.

"Jesus, fuck, Logan."

"Ten grand. Because I know you're about to ask."

"Shit." He stands from his chair and paces the room.

"I'm going to sell my bike," I answer.

"I can help you..." he says, letting his voice drift.

"No way." Standing up, I put my hands up to stop him. "I'm not your responsibility. I'm not a kid anymore, and you've already done enough for me. This is not your problem to fix."

"Doesn't mean I can't help you out." When I look over at him, I can see the words left unsaid. Something about my brother. The debt Murph wants to repay.

"Thank you." I clap him on the shoulder. I don't do this mushy shit. I gotta get out of here.

"If you want any of my extra shifts this week..." he says.

I nod in return. I don't know why he's being so generous to me. It's not his job to fix what I've fucked up. And it only makes me feel worse.

Chapter Twelve

SIERRA

The beach feels quiet today. After grabbing the closest cheesy romance novel on my nightstand and throwing it in a simple bag along with a towel, sunscreen, and a bottle of water, I head to the beach.

I need to just unwind for a day—separate myself from the commotion for a minute. With my parents in my ear pressuring me about who I do and do not fraternize with and then the incident with Logan last night, my head is spinning.

There's a nice, lonely spot on the northern end of the island that is perfect. It's not entirely solitary. There are families and a few locals, but it's not as crazy as the main drag of the beach by the pier.

It's perfect for reading and relaxing.

Too bad I can't focus on the words on the page. I can't stop thinking about Logan last night.

And not just the incident with Murph showing up, talking about the cops.

But also how close we came to finally throwing that little deal we made out the window.

And how freaking good it felt to come so close.

Why am I so crazy for this guy?

Is it really our history? The years and years of curiosity that turned into desire? Or is it something more? I refuse to believe it's as simple as he claims, that I'm just a good girl in need of a rebellion—a little fantasy to fulfill.

That doesn't feel right.

It's more than that. I love how strong he tries to be when I see the tenderness underneath.

How he's always trying to protect me. But also willing to push me. Challenge me. Tease me.

God, am I really falling for this guy? It was supposed to be a spring break fling, but my heart keeps arguing with me, knowing that deep down I want something more.

That if I really had control of my life, I would stay on Wickett forever. I would buy that bookshop from the old lady and run it myself. It wouldn't be the most lucrative business venture, but what do I even need money for here?

But I can't put that kind of pressure on Logan. Would our relationship even stand that kind of commitment? No way would he be down for that.

Maybe it is a fantasy.

Dreams of a girl whose fate has already been decided.

I will go to Yale, like my dad wants. I will meet some white-collar boy there that makes my parents happy. Get married, pop out a few kids, and spend the rest of my years preparing them for the same future.

Round and round it goes.

It sounds suffocating and impossibly miserable.

My mind wanders into dangerous territory...

Imagining Logan standing across the aisle of a quaint beach wedding.

The two of us living under the same small roof, cuddled up every night to watch movies on a tablet because we can't afford a TV.

A warm, fragile baby cradled in those tattoo-covered arms.

Whoa, Sierra. Back the fuck up.

It's a little too crazy to start dreaming stuff like that.

Logan probably doesn't even want kids. He's not a family guy like that.

But maybe...

"Hey there, gorgeous." A voice shocks me out of my near-sleep daze.

I sit up in a jolt, looking up to see a smiling face blocking the sun and creating a silhouette. It takes a moment to recognize the narrow eyes and bright smile of the boy I met the other day, the one who walked me home.

Hale. It takes me a minute to remember his voice. His name—that I learned soon after we met—and number are programmed into my phone, though I never intended on using it.

"Hi," I answer.

"Mind if I join you for a moment?"

Honestly, yes. I do. But I smile and pat the sand next to me instead. Manners, I guess.

"You didn't come to my party," he says, knocking my shoulder with his.

"Oh, I'm sorry. I got stuck hanging out with my parents," I answer, faking a smile.

He's a handsome guy and seems innocent enough. Nice smile and kind eyes.

"Oh, I know how that goes," he laughs. Does he, though? Hale reminds me of the kind of guy who doesn't give half a care about what his parents think. He's the embodiment of entitlement and privilege. His parents probably groomed him to do whatever he wants without a second thought for another living person.

Gosh, I'm grumpy today.

"Do your parents live on the island too?" I ask, taking a swig from my water bottle. I should have put alcohol in it.

"No. I'm here on my own. We used to come for

spring break, like your family, but I fell in love with it, so I stayed."

"Ah," I say, which is a non-answer. I don't know how to respond to this guy. I guess if I really cared what he was talking about I would have a better answer, but as it is, something about him has me on edge. I suddenly wish it was Logan sitting next to me. I sincerely care about what he talks about. I would have all the questions in the world with him.

"Dad wanted me to go to college, and I did manage it for a year, but it wasn't for me. I missed the beach. And the partying." He winks at me. "Ya know?"

"Yeah..." I say. But not really. I'm not a partier, obviously. I'd much rather have a good time with one person than a beach full of doped-up strangers.

"My parents want me to go to college too. I'd rather stay here myself."

I don't know why I tell him that. It feels like the first time I've admitted it.

"You should." His voice is gentle, and there's something intimate about it. Like he wants me to stay with him.

"I'll think about it."

He's watching me, but I keep my eyes on the water.

"Want to go for a swim?" he asks, and I'm about to answer, but then his hand is brushing against my arm, propped in the sand. It nearly chokes me with the way he feels so brazen to touch me.

"I'm good here," I answer. "You can, though." I

squint at him with a smile, and everything feels suddenly so awkward.

"Me too," he echoes as he leans back in the sand the same way I am, elbows dug into the beach towel. It makes me feel suddenly exposed, and I sit up to counteract it.

I pull my knees up to my body and loop my arms around my legs. He turns on his side and faces me. His fingers brush my arm again, then my stomach flips as they slide down the length of my calf. Who the fuck does this guy think he is?

I glance behind me, secretly praying that Logan would be nearby, but I practically go pale when I notice that the nearby families have all left. Other than two or three quiet couples scattered far from us, we are alone. My nerves are on fire and every alarm in my head is telling me to get out of this situation.

"Are you looking for your boyfriend?" he says, and I freeze.

"I don't—" I stammer, but he cuts me off.

"Word travels fast around here, Sierra. I know about you and Logan Woods."

Hearing his full name on Hale's lips makes it hard to breathe. How did I not even know his last name yet? The way he said it has my skin crawling. However he knows Logan, it's not a good relationship, and I can't bear to hear anymore.

"I was just about to leave." I grab my water bottle, readying myself to stand, but he grabs my hand and not in a warm, friendly way.

"If you know what's good for you, you'd stay away from him. Logan's about to go down, and if you get too close, he'll take you down with him."

"Let go of me," I snap at him, quickly jerking my hand away.

He laughs. "You tell that boyfriend of yours that if he doesn't get me my money, he's going to have much bigger problems on his hands than some dealing charges. You want to send him that message for me..."

He eyes me suspiciously, and it makes my stomach turn.

"Or should we send him another message?" He winks, and I grit my teeth at him.

"Logan had nothing to do with Tyler's death. You can try to intimidate him, but you don't scare me." Then, I move to stand, grabbing my towel and bag from the sand.

"Be careful, Sierra. You're just the right amount of leverage someone would need to get Logan right where they want him." His voice is tight and there's something not right about it. It's the first time I realize that he's on something. Not drunk, but something different. Like he's more intense. That he thinks he's stronger and more powerful than he really is.

I take off, scrambling up the beach toward the boardwalk, trying not to gain too much attention. The only thought in my brain is to get to Logan. I won't be safe until I'm in his arms.

LOGAN

My bike is worth at least twelve grand, and if I had the time and freedom to really sell it to someone who would appreciate it, I could get that much. But in my current situation, I'll take ten.

Theo was with me when I bought it. He was the one who tried to talk me out of it, if you could believe it. I realize now that Theo wanted something different for me, to push me away from his way of life, rather than welcome me in, in hopes that I might end up differently.

He told me to get a reasonable car that was good on gas, but I wanted freedom. I wanted the open road and the wind in my face. I wanted something powerful and dangerous because I could make those decisions for myself, for the first time in my life.

No one was going to stop me.

And it feels like I'm selling that freedom away on the internet to a complete stranger right now.

I listed the bike last night on a few indie sale sites, and I woke up to a ton of requests. But not one of these guys really knows what she's worth. Or what she meant to me.

My hand glides across the leather seat. I know I need to message these guys back, but I can't. Something is stopping me.

Murph and I had a long conversation last night about what I need to do. Sell the bike. Be rid of Hale, pay off my debt, and walk away scot-free. And I can't fucking wait for that.

But the cost is more than I can handle right now.

It's making me anxious. Jumpy for something I can't put my finger on.

Murph also seems to think that I should find a way to keep Sierra around. As if that's really an option for me. As if being with me would actually be an improvement in her life.

He doesn't get it.

The crowd is heavy today, but business is slow. I'm just sitting on my bike watching the traffic walk by when a familiar face grabs my attention. She's across the street, but her expression has the hairs on the back of my neck standing at full attention.

Something's wrong.

Fuck.

When she spots me, she takes off in a full run, bolting across the street, making one car slam on his brakes and lay on his horn. I jump out to the street to reach her and give the asshole behind the wheel a piece of my mind.

Sierra buries herself in my arms and breathes into my chest. The rhythm of her breathing changes, and I can tell she's crying.

"What happened?" I try to pull her face away to see if she's hurt. "Baby, look at me."

I'm so on edge, I want to punch something just to make her pain go away. She clearly doesn't want to talk yet, so I pull her over to the shop. She won't leave my side, keeping her face hidden as we shuffle past the lobby toward the back.

Murph is with a client, but he sends me a concerned glance as we pass.

When I finally get her to the bathroom in the back, I manage to get her to splash her face with cool water. It seems to calm her enough to be able to look into my eyes. She no longer has that glossy stare, like she's looking through me.

"Please talk to me," I whisper, brushing away the hair that's stuck to the sweat on her face.

"It was this guy, someone I met. He found me on the beach. Told me you owe him money, that you have to pay...or...or...I don't know."

I can feel the seething rage boil under my skin, and I'm already in a mood to kill a motherfucker.

"I didn't want to let him get under my skin. I hate that he scares me, but, Logan, he scared me," she starts to sob so I pull her into a hug again.

My vision is gone. I only see red.

"Did you catch his name?" I ask.

She sniffles and pulls away to mutter, "Hale."

Fuck.

"I think he was on something. He just looked weird," she mumbles into my shirt.

"You're safe now," I say, my lips against her head, but

I can't help but wonder if she is. What did I think was going to happen? He needed a bargaining chip against me, and he found one.

"I didn't tell him anything, Logan. I tried to get out of there as fast as possible."

My heart breaks into a million little pieces hearing her cry to me like this. Like she thought I would be mad at her. Like anything she could have done would warrant some little shit on the beach to treat her like this.

Fuck, I'm going to jail. Once I leave her here with Murph, I'm going to find that little fuck somehow, and I'm going to beat the snot out of him in front of everyone. And I'll be in jail.

Then prison, because I'm still on probation.

But it will be so fucking worth it.

"Are you okay? Do you want me to take you home?" I look at her face again.

"No," she bursts out quickly.

Then, she looks up at me with an expression of terror. "Logan, don't do anything. I don't want you getting hurt. Just let it go."

The moment grows silent as she watches me, looking for any sign that I won't do anything crazy.

And the blood-red heat I felt a moment ago goes icy-cold. How did I not see this coming? The sight of her and Hale standing together outside of her building the other day flashes in my mind. I'm frozen in place.

Sierra's arms wrap tightly around my waist, and she

squeezes my body against hers.

I brush her hair out of her face and lean down to press my lips against her forehead. How does this girl have such an effect on me? She touches something deep down inside of me, something familiar but so old I've forgotten it exists.

Murph lets me take Sierra back to my apartment to let her settle down. She doesn't want to go home; she is really adamant about that. And I can understand. Not wanting to get her parents involved.

When we get back to my place, I let her lay down on the bed while I make her something to eat. My apartment might be small, but at least it's well stocked. So, I quickly put some water on to boil pasta to pair with a garlic cream sauce that my brother taught me to make. It's turned into my specialty.

Before I know it, I can hear her heavy breathing from the bed. She must have fallen asleep pretty quickly from the rush of adrenaline. It can do that to you. I have experience there.

While I'm cooking in the kitchen, the sky outside opens up and lets down a heavy pour that hits the windows. That, with the fading light creates the most serene environment, so once I finish the sauce and pasta, I put it in the oven to stay warm. Then I creep gently in the bed behind Sierra, and before I know it, I'm out too.

Chapter Thirteen

SIERRA

I wake to the feeling of heavy arms around my waist. It's pitch-black, and the most delicious aroma fills the room.

I don't know what time it is. And I don't care.

Squeezing his arms around me, I savor the warmth and comfort I feel when I'm with him. You don't feel like that when it's just a fling. This is more than that, and I need to come to terms with it.

When I'm with Logan, I am more myself than when I'm around my parents or friends from back home. He lets me be me.

He must feel me fidget because he squeezes me back, nuzzling his face into my neck and letting out a low growl that makes my skin erupt in goosebumps.

"Dinner's ready," he mumbles.

"Is that a euphemism?"

His low rumble of laughter hums through my body. I twist myself until I'm facing him, and his eyes open to stare into mine. There's just enough light to see his blue eyes in the darkness. His hand comes up to rest on my cheek, and I keep my hands on his chest.

For a few moments we don't say anything.

We're hiding away from the chaos of the week to just be alone and safe together. The encounter with Hale is still on my mind, but I feel helpless in the matter. The image he painted of Logan doesn't match the man in front of me. I want to help him, at least with his debts, but I know better than to offer to solve his problems for him. Logan would shut that down so fast...

But if I could stick around, then maybe things would change for him.

"I don't want to leave," I whisper.

He's quiet. I didn't mean to really let this out just yet, but it slipped. Something about the fragile tension between us made me want to spill my secrets.

"You mean Wickett?" His voice is gravelly and quiet.

"Yeah."

I wait for his response. Something, anything that tells me to stay. I know that with one word, I would do it. I would stay. I'm too vulnerable and desperate for anything to hold on to.

And he doesn't answer, just rolls away and sits up with his feet on the floor and his head in his hands.

I have to swallow down my nerves. I've grown too attached, and it's pushing him away.

"Logan," I whisper, sitting up and placing my hand on his back.

He quickly stands and walks toward the kitchen area, flipping on a bright light that chases away the delicate mood in the room. I watch as he pulls a pan out of the oven and gives it a little stir before tasting it.

"What did I say?" I ask.

"Nothing. Are you hungry?" He's put up a wall between us. His voice is cold and distant as he pulls down a couple bowls and starts filling them with a creamy white pasta.

My breathing gets shallow from frustration.

In a leap, I stomp across the room and put myself in his line of sight. "Logan, stop it."

He drops the bowl on the counter with a thud. "You can't talk like that," he barks at me.

"Talk like what? About staying?" I can't believe he's shutting down on me so much over this.

"Yes. About staying."

"Why? Why is it so bad that I want to stay here?"

His mouth is closed tightly as he avoids my question again. He's still trying to fix the food, but my nerves are so on edge, my stomach couldn't handle anything right now.

"It's because you don't want me." My voice shakes, and I can't help the tears that are following. "I get it. This is just a fun fling for you, but it feels like a lot more than that to me, Logan." I place myself between him and the counter, steeling myself against his words. "If you don't want me, tell me now so I don't fall even harder when this week is over."

His hands are on the counter, framing me between them. His head drops as I wait for the words that will ruin me. Waiting for him to tell me to leave. That I got too attached, too clingy. That I let my emotions get too involved and ruined everything.

"Oh, Sierra," he murmurs.

"Just tell me, Logan. Tell me you don't care about me, and I'll leave now. Spare me from the heartache."

He's so still. His jaw is clenched tight, and I can see the movement in his muscles holding his mouth closed.

"That's not it, is it?" I whisper, letting my hands slide up the sides to his face. "Please talk to me."

"You can't stay here, Sierra."

"Don't you want me?" I beg.

In one motion, his discipline dissolves, and he loops his arm around my waist, pulling me against his body. The other hand grips the back of my head, putting my face level with his.

"Of course, I want you. Of course, I want you to stay. I should tell you to leave, don't you understand? If I had any balls, I would have sent you away right now. Break your heart now before I ruin your life."

Then he kisses me. It's a hungry, passionate devouring of each other. It's not the kind of kiss that leads to anything else, but the kind that settles our doubts.

It's the kind of kiss that says he wants me to stay.

LOGAN

I'm so fucking weak. When I was given the chance to save her, push her away so that she could live a happy life without me, I caved.

I couldn't stand the sight of her thinking that I wouldn't want her. That anyone wouldn't want her. It's insanity.

The truth faces me like a bright light now. I want Sierra more than I have ever wanted anything.

Holding her in my arms feels like I'm not such a piece of shit. Like I could make her happy. Keep her safe.

We finally pull away from our heated kiss, and it's so hard to let her out of my grasp. I need to feed her something. After the day she's had, she needs to eat.

So I make her sit down and put the warm bowl of pasta in front of her. When she takes a bite, her eyelids flutter and she makes a soft moan.

It does things to me.

"This is delicious, Logan." She devours one bowl in no time, so I scoop another helping for her before starting on my own.

"I'm glad you like it."

"Where did you learn to cook?"

"My brother taught me," I answer, my voice clipped. I can feel her watching me.

"You don't want to talk about him." She says it as a fact, but I can sense the question there.

No better time than now. If I really want her to stay, I need to think about opening up at some point.

"He died two years ago."

Her rapt attention is on me now, her face softer, and her lips parted just slightly.

"We grew up in foster homes together. So when he came here, I followed closely behind. And he made a nice home for us. It was the first time I really had a home. A proper family. He got me a job at the shop because he knew I had a talent for drawing. I saved up enough money to buy my bike. For a couple years, it was really nice."

My voice lets out a little quiver in the last word. Shit. I do not want to start getting emotional. Why is talking about this so hard?

Her soft hand reaches out and squeezes mine, and my eyes find hers.

"How did he die?" she breathes.

I swallow.

The words won't come. I can't say them. Not out

loud.

But she squeezes my hand again. To reassure me. And suddenly I'm not alone.

"Overdose."

My vision goes blurry and it takes me by surprise. What the fuck?

And when I blink, my cheeks feel wet, and I want to hate myself for crying in front of her, but she doesn't even react. She just brushes her thumb across my cheek and wipes the tears away.

Clearing my throat, I quickly try to shut the emotions down.

I want her to say something because I don't trust myself to speak, and I hate that last word spoken so much. And it's just hanging in the air, souring my mood.

"Logan, I'm so sorry."

Her expression changes. It's more than just sympathy...there's confusion in her brow.

"But I don't understand...if he...then why would you still...?"

And I get it. From an outsider's perspective. If my brother died of an overdose, why would I still sell it and use it? Logically, it's incoherent. But there is no logic where grief and addiction are involved.

"I don't have a good answer for that." I stand up and walk away, clearing the dishes. I know that I need to tell her to leave Wickett. That I'm an addict and always will be. That she deserves so much better, but when I turn back to look at her, she's already looking at me, and I fucking love the way she looks at me. Like she sees something no one else sees. Like she was made to look at me and that I might not be a worthless piece of shit, after all.

"It's late," I mumble, looking back at her.

"It's only eight," she whispers.

"The bargain we made still stands." I blurt it out for some godforsaken reason. As on edge as my nerves feel right now, I have to remind myself that nothing has really changed. Sierra can't stay with me forever. This is essentially still a fling, and I can't change that.

But then again...we do still have some parameters in this bargain.

Like she can read my mind, Sierra stands up and saunters over, her eyes full of lust.

"I think the bed is a bad idea." There goes my stupid mouth again.

"I don't care where we go. I just want to be with you." She reaches up on her toes and kisses me, unleashing that power inside of me. I latch onto her mouth with mine, pressing my tongue between her lips and against her tongue.

She lets out a warm, sweet moan against my mouth. My hands wrap around her thighs and lift her against my body. She's so warm, so soft and light in my arms. I could get used to this.

I'm so hard already, aching to ease the pressure and dive into that sweet spot. Mine. A small voice inside howls.

That's a new feeling.

The more I feel the warmth of her sex against my body, the more it echoes to claim her. Make her mine.

I can't do that, though. My mind has blocked all prospects of going all the way with Sierra, especially after how attached she's growing. Sex would only make it that much harder to let her go.

But that doesn't mean I can't still give her the pleasure I'm so desperate to give. Walking over to the bed, I set her down gently and she immediately starts with my pants, like she's just picking up where we left off yesterday. Quickly, I hold her fingers with my hand, stopping her from doing something that can't be undone.

Instead, I drop onto my knees and trail my fingers up the sides of her thighs to reach the strings of her bikini bottoms under her see-through swim cover. I feel her tremble as I pull them down, lifting her gently off the bed as I do.

"Logan," she breathes through parted lips.

I answer her back with kisses along the insides of her thighs where the skin is so soft and the aroma of her sex draws me in.

Sierra's body is my alter, and I want to worship. To repent for my sins.

Placing her hands behind her, she lets her head fall back with a moan just as I run my tongue across her warm folds, feeling her tense at the contact, then relax into the pleasure.

She gasps for air, so I don't stop. When I cover her with my mouth, teasing that sweet spot of pleasure at the top, she explodes with a high-pitched yelp. Her legs tighten around my head as I continue to tease her clit, never easing on the pressure or the pulse.

I am desperate to make her come. Her pleasure is everything to me at this moment. There is no addiction here, no threat, no danger. Only making the most beautiful person I know feel like she is flying on a fucking cloud. If I can do that much, then maybe I'm not so fucking terrible.

Gently, I slide one finger in, and she drops onto the mattress, arching her back as she continues to gasp for air.

"Oh God, Logan," she whines. "I'm gonna come."

My dick pulses in my pants, and I can feel my own orgasm coming on as I slide another finger in with barely enough room, pushing her closer and closer to ecstasy.

"Come for me, Sierra," I moan against her sex.

Then, I pick up speed, curling my fingers to find just the right pleasure spot. She's writhing on my bed, and it's honestly the most beautiful thing I have ever seen. I suck her clit with even more pressure, teasing the fuck out of it with every flick of my tongue, and as soon as I feel myself crashing into an orgasm, Sierra screams.

Her hands dig into my hair as her legs stiffen up next

to my ears. Her body quakes through the orgasm, small spasms cascading down her legs until she finally collapses with a long sigh.

I don't want to leave her, my mouth never wants to come up for air, but I let her relax as I place a last kiss against her inner thigh. Then, I gently pull her bikini bottoms back up and move up to trail kisses along her legs, her stomach, and her neck.

Not quite sure how she'd feel about a mouth kiss, I'm a little surprised that she grabs my face and smashes her lips against mine, running her tongue against my lips. And just the thought of her tasting herself would have me coming again if I hadn't already released my load in my pants.

This girl is exquisite and I don't deserve her.

Chapter fourteen

SIERRA

The shitty events of the day aside, I went to bed last night on cloud nine. Logan was the cure to all of my anxiety and insecurities. The way he comforted me when I was upset was all about being there, not buying me something or shoving my pain aside.

I woke up this morning with a smile on my face, remembering that moment on his bed when he shattered my reality and completely opened my eyes to what pleasure could be. Walking away from Logan is going to be impossible, which is why I'm still forging a plan to avoid it at all costs.

My parents are taking me to breakfast today. We always come to the diner at least once every spring break for the greasy hash browns and bacon. My parents think it's cute to indulge in the local dives at least once on our trip, like it's a novelty or something. In reality, this place is packed full of tourists and locals alike.

When we walk in, I spot his brightly-colored tattoos before anything else. He's sitting at the bar sipping his black coffee over a plate of scrambled eggs. I bite my lips seeing his fingers wrapped around the ceramic coffee mug, remembering fondly what those fingers did to me yesterday, and the pleasure strikes a nerve low in my belly.

"Party of three," my mother says to the hostess, and he must recognize her voice because Logan turns immediately and locks eyes with me as I follow my parents to our booth. He won't be introducing himself or inviting himself to dine with us, but he does send me a subtle wink and a barely noticeable lift at the corner of his mouth.

Damn, he is so sexy.

I want to drag him off that barstool and make him do very dirty things to me in the back of the restaurant.

My cheeks start to flush just thinking about it. His hands up my skirt, his lips on my neck—

"Sierra."

I glance up and see my parents staring at me. I was really daydreaming because I didn't even hear the waitress ask for my drink order.

"Just water, please," I answer.

"You've been a busy bee lately," my mother says as she pours two packets of sugar into her coffee. "Where were you off to?"

Swallowing, I try to catch a sideways glance at Logan as I say, "Just hanging out with a new friend."

I catch the way he turns his head, peeking over at us without directly looking. He can easily hear our conversation.

My mom and dad share a quick, furtive glance at each other just before they lift their menus to cover their faces. "Not locals, I hope," my dad says, loud enough for at least half of the restaurant to hear.

"Dad," I whisper-shout at him.

"Your dad is just worried about you getting caught up with the trouble around here. These small communities can be so easily plagued with drugs and crime, Sierra." My mom has the sense to be a little quieter about it, but I still grow hot, knowing that Logan can hear everything. Quickly, I glance at him. He's turned back to face his breakfast, but I spot the clenching of his jaw.

I want to argue with them, but I don't know what to say.

"Stick with our friends and your regular group of friends here, darling," my dad adds.

"Oh, you mean Natalie Reed?" I ask with a laugh. If only they knew the people Natalie associated with and her spring break behavior. How I was nearly attacked because I chose to hang out with her.

"Keep your voice down," my dad chides me.

"You keep your voice down," I mimic. He doesn't mind insulting the locals, but the minute I bring up his law partner's delinquent daughter, he gets upset.

"You're ruining breakfast," my mother says coldly, hiding behind her menu.

When the waitress returns, we grow quiet along with the rest of the diner. I quickly order a veggie omelet as I try to watch Logan who seems to be done with his breakfast.

Please don't leave. I hate to think about the space without him in it. Without him to look at. That feeling I get when he's not around, although so new, I already hate it.

"Sierra, tell us more about your friend," my dad commands, not out of curiosity, but out of obligation.

Sitting up and taking a deep breath, I tell him. "I met him at the big bonfire on the first night. He's...a gentleman, and we're having a great week. Probably my favorite trip to Wickett so far."

"He sounds nice," my mother says with an easy smile on her face.

"Do we know his parents?" my dad adds, and I freeze up.

Logan is waiting for me to answer the question, to tell him that he's a local, not a trust fund kid with a timeshare. But if I come out with the truth now, it will compromise all of our time together for our remaining few days, and more importantly, it will ruin all of my plans to find a way to stay. I want to tell Logan all of that, but I know he's just waiting to hear me come clean.

"No..." I mumble. "You don't know his parents."

"Is it serious?" my mom asks, piercing me with her curious stare.

I have to clear my throat. It feels like I'm suffocating with these questions. Why did I bring this up? There is way too much riding on this plan of mine that I suddenly feel overwhelmed with the need to just hide Logan and all of my dreams away, safe from anyone who might ruin them.

"I think so."

My mom and dad both sit up straighter, like they both expected an easy no.

In the corner of my eye, I can see Logan freeze up. Then he drops a bill on the counter and waves to the waitress as he moves toward the door. I can't help but watch him, begging him to look at me. Give me one glance so I know that I'm not screwing this up.

"We'd love to meet him," my mother adds, but I'm barely listening. All of my attention is on that gorgeous tattooed man walking through the door and away from me without even a glance, and my gut turns with worry that this was all too real for him.

"Excuse me. I see someone I know." I burst out of my seat and out the front door. My mother says my name as I run through the door and down the boardwalk toward the shop. Logan didn't get far. He's only on the crosswalk ahead.

"Logan," I call for him. He turns to see me as if I've offended him.

When I reach where he's stopped, he quickly pulls me into the alcove of an empty store front, hiding us from view of the restaurant.

Without another word, I launch onto my toes to press my mouth to his. He tastes like salt and coffee and Logan, and I want to know the familiarity of him for the rest of my life. I want to kiss him after every breakfast.

He kisses back hungrily, but after a moment, he pulls back. Pushing me away at the hips. "You should go back to your parents, Sierra."

"I don't want to," I whisper against his lips.

"Stop saying that," he answers. "You heard them. They were right. There is crime and drugs here, and I don't want you getting mixed up with all of that."

"I trust you," I answer, trying to pull him back to me.

"I am the criminal they are talking about. I'm the problem, Sierra. You deserve so much better than me."

"I'm falling for you, Logan. I don't have a choice."

He freezes, looking into my eyes and searching for the truth. I am falling for him. Hell, I've already fallen. I never want to be away from him again. Logan is my future.

LOGAN

Seeing Sierra with her parents brought a whole new sense of reality to this situation. No matter what happens between Sierra and I, they will always be there. It's just another reminder that we are from different worlds and could never exist together.

Now she's telling me she's falling for me, and all I can think is that my time is running out. Time with her. Time to pay my debt. My life has boiled down to these last two days and how much of it I can save before it's too late.

And right now, my only priority is to keep her safe before it all implodes and drags her down too. I grip the soft cotton of her light blue dress and push her away.

"Listen to me, Sierra. I can't keep you safe, not safe enough. That business with Hale is worse than you think."

"How bad could it be?" she asks, pulling herself closer.

"I can't tell you."

"Why not? Let me help you, Logan. My dad is a lawyer—"

"No. I am not getting you any more involved than you already are, and your parents aren't interested in helping me."

"If they knew how much you meant to me..."

"It would be in their best interest to let me end up in jail, Sierra. Don't you understand? They don't want their daughter with a drug dealer. A criminal. An addict."

She reaches for me again, and this time I move away before she can touch me.

It's time for some damage control. I had been pushing away the fact that Hale was pursuing Sierra, that he was with her yesterday, threatening her. It's time to scare Sierra away...for good.

Turning back in a fit of frustration, I push her against the wall of the storefront as I say, "Did you think Hale was bluffing yesterday?"

She's staring at me with her eyebrows fixed downward and her crystal blue gaze trained directly on me.

"He's using you to get back at me, Sierra. I owe him a lot of money, and if I don't get it back to him by Sunday, he's going to have me thrown in jail...or worse. And he's threatening you to get at me."

I watch the color drain from Sierra's face as her hand drifts up to cover her neck.

"But you didn't do anything..."

"I owe him ten grand, which he probably pays most of to someone even scarier than him. Someone who won't hesitate to frame an innocent guy for murder. Or kidnap a pretty young girl to find other ways to make that money back."

She shakes her head and steps backward, away from

me. That's what I wanted her to do, but it still hurts.

"I know you trust me, Sierra, but I cannot protect you. I can hardly protect myself. And if I can't guarantee your safety, then you have to leave me. Tell your parents you're ready to go home. Get off Wickett, and forget about me."

Sierra's face is blank, like she's thinking through the events of the week, all the times I kept her around when I could have warned her. All the times I put her in danger for my own selfish desire to be near her.

"Fine," she whispers as she steps away.

I don't bother apologizing; that would only make her want to stay. I can do nothing but watch her go and convince myself that this was what I wanted.

Chapter fifteen

SIERRA

My mind is racing after I walk away from Logan. I knew he was in debt, and I could tell he's under a lot of stress, but the fear I saw in his eyes has me shook. Ten grand is a lot more than I expected.

Feeling like a pawn is not what I wanted out of this week, and it draws up a strange feeling of anger, but there's something else there too. Resentment.

Hale underestimated me if he thought I could be played as a hostage for Logan's debt. He must think I'm just a stupid rich girl, but he is so very wrong.

As I return to the table to continue breakfast with my parents, I keep that image of Hale on the beach in my head, knowing that if I saw him again, I would turn the tables on him. Threaten him with my dad's law firm, use him to garner as much information as possible until I had him exactly where I wanted him, enough to get him to let Logan go free of his debt. I could keep Logan safe.

When I walk into the restaurant, the first thing I notice is that the food must have come while I was gone because Mom is putting a piece of bacon in her mouth with a smile. Then I notice that my parents are not alone. A blond-haired man is sitting next to my mom, at first blocked by my dad's head.

"There she is," my mother calls toward me. With the next step toward the table, my heart drops into my gut when I stare directly at the familiar blond-haired boy I was just thinking about. He's giving me a sly, crooked smile as I approach, feeling stunned and sick seeing him with my parents, especially after what I know now.

He stands up and takes my hand, and I nearly slap it away, wanting to claw his eyes out, but he takes my hand in his and pulls me close to place a kiss on my cheek. Just when I start to pull away, he grips my hand tighter and leans his mouth against my ear.

"It's so nice to meet your parents," he whispers. "Your secret is safe with me."

When I pull away and glare at him, he gives me a quick wink, and I realize what secret he's talking about. Logan's secret.

It turns out that Hale beat me to it. Instead of having him where I want him, he has me right where he wants me.

"Sierra, you didn't tell us you were inviting your new friend to lunch," my mom squeals, giving Hale another bright smile.

I slowly sit across from him, letting my mind process this new situation. To my parents, Hale is perfect. He is exactly who they want for me.

"It was a surprise," Hale says, taking a sip of his coffee. "Eat up, sweetheart." He pushes my plate toward me, and I can't speak. I can hardly move. How did he know they were my parents? How did he know where we would be?

"Hale was just telling us how much his family owns here on Wickett, and here I thought all the locals were old retired surfers." My dad breaks out in a laugh that Hale overenthusiastically joins.

I stare out the window, watching for Logan, wishing I could run out to him now. Can he see us? How can I get a message to him?

"Eat up, Sierra," my mother says. "Your father and I have a twelve o'clock tee time."

"Hale, you guys want to join us for nine rounds?" My dad smiles at the boy sitting across from me, and my stomach twists. I think I might actually be sick.

"No, thank you. I actually have a little afternoon surprise planned for Sierra," he looks at me with a wink and smile as he takes a bite of my omelet.

A thick lump builds in my throat. Fear has me completely paralyzed, and the thought of being alone with him makes my eyes prick with threatening tears. But I push them away. He has too much on Logan. I have to play the part for him.

"You feeling okay, Sierra?" my mom asks.

Pressing a forced smile across my face, I shove a bite of eggs into my mouth. Then, I nod. "Yeah, I'm just a little nervous to see what he has planned."

"You're going to love it," he adds, and that single bite of food threatens to come back up.

Hale pays for breakfast, privately of course, which makes my parents fawn over him even more. He has money, which must be the only thing that matters to them. As we walk out of the restaurant, my skin pricks with terror. My parents kiss me goodbye and hug Hale before walking away.

He puts an arm around me and takes me in the opposite direction.

We're out of earshot when he starts. "Good girl."

"Why are you doing this?" I ask, pushing back the tears again.

"Call it an insurance policy," he says as he presses his lips against my head. I jerk my head away, but he only squeezes me closer. "I can't have you bringing your daddy into this, making things all messy for me. And in return, I won't have your boyfriend framed for murder."

"You sold Tyler those drugs, and that's what killed

him." We're alone on the boardwalk when Hale press-es me against the wall, acting like we're about to kiss when he threatens me, his harsh voice in my ear. "You keep talking like that, sweetheart, and your boyfriend will fry. It won't be hard for me to have him put away for this. He fits the bill."

"You won't get away with it," I answer back.

"You have no evidence against me, Sierra. There's nothing you could use to incriminate me, so don't even try. Keep your daddy on my side, and your boy-friend stays out of jail."

Pushing him away, he finally relents and backs off, pulling me with him. "Come on, darling," he says as he puts my arm around him again. A couple approaches down the boardwalk, and I quickly realize that I can't make a scene so I let him hold me close as we con-tinue walking.

"I have to get back to work," he says finally, and I'm so relieved that he's letting me go. "But I want to see you tomorrow. Just to make sure everything is still good with you. How about you go see that boyfriend of yours and remind him of how much he owes me. Then you can deliver it at sundown, by the bonfire."

"What if he doesn't have it?" I ask, already knowing the answer.

"I think you know, baby." He plants another kiss against my head, and again I push him away. Stepping away from him, he pats me on the butt. Quickly, he pulls me back before I can breathe in my freedom.

"I almost forgot." He pulls his phone out of his back pocket and puts me in a chokehold, holding me close to his body. Then, he points the camera on us as he licks the side of my face while hitting the button and capturing the picture of my misery.

Finally, he lets me go. "See you tomorrow, beautiful. Oh, and, Sierra," he barks at me. I turn toward him with my teeth gritted and my brow furrowed. "You and only you tomorrow, baby."

Then, he winks.

Without another thought, I take off toward the shop.

LOGAN

The smiling faces of the people on the front of the pamphlet are staring up at me as if they know something I don't. And maybe they do. The secret of sobriety isn't much of a secret, I want to tell them. Everyone knows it's a far better life. It's not a matter of choice, it's a matter of control.

And we're living our lives without it.

Murph has been sneaking these pamphlets into my station for months. He doesn't want to come right out and say it, but I can tell he's trying to be as subtle about it as possible. He probably still feels guilty over how things went down with Theo—how none of us knew the truth. He hid his addiction so well, that the most any of us really knew was that he occasionally liked to let loose. After he died, we cleaned out the apartment to find evidence of it everywhere. Right under our noses all along.

I'm sitting in the back of the shop while Murph finishes up a tatt on a military guy here on R&R—for free, of course. Murph never charges active duty guys, not after his ten years in the service. He just wasn't the same guy when he came back.

Sierra's face when I scared her this morning keeps replaying in my head. She needed to know the severity of the situation. I owed her that much.

My phone pings from my pocket, and I open it to find a message from the marketplace app that Murph helped me list my bike on.

Will you take $8,000?

I roll my eyes. The nerve of these people. It's an insult.

It's worth far more than what I'm asking. 10 is the lowest I'll go.

Because ten grand is what I owe my supplier, but I'm not going to tell him that. Truth be told, I'm desperate to sell it, but dreading the affirmative reply that comes a minute later.

I'll take it. Can I come check it out in the morning?

Heaving a heavy sigh, I answer with my location and a good time. Then, I peer back at the pamphlet on my lap. At first, I try to convince myself that this will be a fresh start. Debt-free. Drug-free.

Sierra-free.

It hardly feels like a new beginning and more like a bitter end. Even if I do get my life together, she'll still be too good for me.

Suddenly, my phone pings again. Expecting it to be the buyer again, I'm nearly shocked off my stool when there is a picture of Hale and Sierra on my phone. He's got his arm tight around her neck and his tongue against her cheek. The look of terror on her face makes my skin crawl.

"Everything okay?" Murph calls from the front of the shop.

I don't respond. I can't exactly say yes.

A pounding at the back door makes me jump again.

"Logan!" Her familiar voice has me pulling the door open in a panic. Sierra is standing at the back door, looking distressed and scared out of her mind. Without hesitation, I pull her into my arms and look around for any sign of Hale behind her. But she seems to be alone.

"He found me," she stammers. "He was with my parents."

"I'm sorry," I whisper into her hair.

It was a warning. To show just how much power he has and how much he owns me. If anything, it was further proof that my time working for Hale is over. I'm selling my bike and giving him the money, and I'm done.

Quickly, I pull out my phone and text the guy on the marketplace app.

Any chance you could come today?

Chapter Sixteen

SIERRA

"I hope you're done pushing me away now," I say to him over my cup of coffee.

We're sitting two doors down in the almost empty bookshop. The small coffee shop in the back gives us enough privacy to talk.

"I never should have let you get this involved." His head is hanging, so I reach out and intertwine my fingers with his.

"Well I am, so now we can get through this together."

When he lifts his head, I get lost in those piercing

blues again. His eyes are full of remorse. So I join him on the small couch and pull his face up to mine. Kissing his lips slowly, I try to make him feel this connection between us. That we are stronger together and that I won't leave so easily.

His phone pings in his lap, so we slowly pull apart. After looking down, his features harden again. "He's here," he says as he stands.

"Want me to come with you?" I ask.

"Nah," he answers as leans down to drop a kiss on the top of my head.

Then, he walks out of the bookstore to sell his beloved motorcycle to a complete stranger. The broken-hearted expression on his face breaks my heart. I want to fix all of this for him, tell him it will be a new beginning, a clean start, but he's already out the front door.

"Can I take these for you?" the old woman asks, interrupting me from my daze.

"Oh, please let me," I say as I pick up our cups and plates and take them to the counter. "May I?" I ask, gesturing to the sink. "I could really use something to occupy my mind."

"Help yourself," she says as she backs away toward the front of the store.

"Thank you." Then, I walk behind the counter and start cleaning our dishes in the sink. The water is so hot it nearly burns my hands, but the burn feels good. It distracts me from the other insane thoughts in my head right now. Thoughts like how much I would love my life if I could work in this bookstore every day. Thoughts like hosting open mic nights and book readings by local authors. Thoughts like going home to Logan every night.

It doesn't take me nearly long enough to wash our few dirty dishes. When I finish, I clean up the sink and help to tidy up a few other things in the kitchen.

"I wish I could afford to pay you. I could really use your help around here." Mrs. Walker comes back with a few pieces of trash left around the store, and I can see by the way she holds her back that she's getting far too old to handle this business by herself.

"I wish I could stay," I answer. "If I could, I'd work for free." Sending her a warm smile, I let my mind get dangerously close to that reality again. My original plan was to stay in the rental property and help my parents rent it out on a vacation rental site, but what if I could stay on Wickett to run this store? It would be far more permanent...if I was ready for that.

"If you could stay, I would give it to you, dear." I look up at the woman, wondering how serious she is. I would never take the business for free, but I do have enough in my savings account to buy it. If she's really serious about selling...

Just then, the front door opens. My eyes shoot up to the door, but it's just a customer wanting to browse. Behind the woman, I see Logan through the slowly closing door. The frown on his face draws me out of the store.

"I'll be right back," I say to the old woman.

When I get outside, Logan lifts his worried eyes up to me. The man, a young guy with a military cut, is sitting on his motorcycle. The one that we rode together just a few days prior to a secluded part of the beach where we shared our first kiss.

I wrap my arms around Logan's waist as he touches his lips to the side of my head. Then, the man starts up the bike, and I feel Logan wince. A moment later, the bike is rolling away, and the man shouts a thanks to us as he waves goodbye.

Logan doesn't move for a moment. So I squeeze him a little tighter, hoping to love the pain out of him. He wraps his arms back around me and pulls me into his body as I feel him breathe a heavy sigh.

"I'm sorry," I whisper against the soft skin of his neck.

"It's okay," he whispers back. "Clean slate, right?"

When he pulls away, I look up into his eyes and see a totally different guy than the one I met just a few days ago. There's a little more hope there than before. He leans down and kisses me slowly, and I let myself feel a touch of hope too. Prospects of owning the bookstore and staying here on Wickett seem so much more reachable.

"I promised Murph I would go to a thing tonight," he mumbles, finally. "I don't want you walking around Wickett alone, though. Just lay low until this is over with tomorrow."

"Don't worry about me. Tonight is the family gathering with my parents at the country club, the only night they 'let me come with them.'"

"Okay, good," he answers. "Stay with them all night. Meet me here bright and early?"

"You got it," I answer, reaching up to kiss him again. I could kiss him endlessly.

LOGAN

There's an aching emptiness without my motorcycle keys in my hands. But more importantly, my mind can't erase that image of Sierra in Hale's grip, the terror on her face. I should never have gotten her involved in all of this, but if she's already involved, then it's up to me to handle it, end it, and keep her safe.

I walk her back to her apartment to be completely sure she's home safe. She promised she would stay with her parents all night, and it gave me a small amount of peace to know that he had no reason to threaten her anymore.

It was late afternoon when I finally got back to my apartment. Murph's pamphlet kept taunting me, telling me to go, only to convince me that I would never be free and that I should just stay home. Finally, telling the voices to fuck off, I grabbed a jacket and walked out the front door.

When I reach the church, I want to leave more than ever. This feels fake. I don't belong here. There is a small group of people hovering around a table inside the poorly lit event room. Just like in every movie I've ever seen, there are brown folding chairs situated in a circle.

When I walk in, the door behind me closes—loudly.

Everyone turns and all eyes are on me. Kill me.

It only takes a second before an old woman with frizzy brown hair and a brightly-colored floral dress smiles, an ear-to-ear grin. She walks over and puts her hand out.

"Hi, hon. Welcome to NA. I'm Esther." Her voice is as weathered and aged as the features of her face. But her smile is genuine, and I actually crack a small smile in return.

"Logan," I mumble in return.

"Come in, babe," she rasps as she pulls me gently by the hand. I get the feeling she could feel my inclination to bolt, and she's physically holding me to her.

The rest of the group greets me as I head toward the styrofoam cups to get some much-needed caffeine. I instantly recognize one of the older guys that I remember selling to a few months back. He teaches at the community college and was always drunk when I met him. I guess now I know why he stopped texting me. He gives me a stern, tight-lipped expression, probably skeptical of my intentions in the group.

After a few forgettable introductions, we take our

seats around the circle. The group seems pretty laid-back, only six of us in total. Esther runs the group and they go through a quick round of updates and announcements, when a young woman with telltale scars on her cheeks cheerfully declares that she's been sober for eighteen months and her kids will come home this summer.

The whole thing is...well, excuse the pun, but it's sobering. Really fucking sobering.

Everyone around the circle is a different age, a different race, gender. A couple carry designer bags while the lady next to me has holes in her shirt and drinks off-brand cola.

When Esther looks at me, I can tell she's expecting me to say something. I walked in here with the promise to myself that I was not going to spill my story; I wasn't going to do the hand-holding kumbaya bullshit.

"Logan, care to introduce yourself? If you're ready, hon."

I love her terms of endearment.

So, I raise my hand up and look at each of the people sitting around me. "My name is Logan. I've been using for over a year now...since—" I clear my throat. "Since my brother died. He overdosed. I mean, I used before that...here and there, but when he died, I really laid into it, you know?"

A few of them nod their heads, letting their eyes avert, probably thinking about some shitty fucking thing that happened to them that made them want to bury reality in a warm blanket and forget their lives altogether.

"Then I met someone. I want it to be serious, but it won't be. Because I'm not the guy she deserves right now." Again, they nod their heads, and then a thought about Sierra occurs to me.

"I haven't gotten high in five days, and I feel like shit, physically. But then I see a version of myself that could actually get a girl like her, and I've never wanted to be clean so much. She's leaving in a few days. What if I give up again? What if when she's gone I don't have anyone to get clean for?"

A hand touches my shoulder, and when I look up, everyone is looking at me. Esther is smiling. "I'm so glad you're here, Logan."

I nod my head in return. "Me too."

Chapter Seventeen

Sierra

When I walk into the annual country club gala, I nearly vomit. What was normally a bougie cocktail party has suddenly become some sort of benefit. Tyler's face, mounted on a canvas taller than me, greets me as I walk in. He is smiling in his teal polo shirt on a yacht with his dad. The sound of his voice growling in my ear comes shuddering back in my memory. Sweat beads on my forehead. I can still feel his tight grip on my arm and his alcohol-laced breath on the skin of my neck.

My parents parade me around the party like they always do. They talk to their friends about me like I'm not even there, remarking on how beautiful I am, how grown up I've gotten, and how my dad should lock me up before I'm corrupted. Normally, I can at least manage a small smile and the bare minimum of cordiality, but my mother starts to notice how cold and lifeless I'm acting.

After about an hour of showing me off like I'm some sort of AKC Pomeranian, she pulls me aside and snaps in a low whisper.

"What are you on?" Her nails bite into the flesh of my arm.

My face twists into confusion. "What?"

"You seem to have misplaced your manners. I can

only assume you're high as a kite right now, so you better sober up and start acting like a polite young lady."

"I'm not on anything," I snarl.

"Then what in God's name is wrong with you?"

Just then, a glass starts clinking as the people at the front of the room gather everyone's attention. A tan-skinned man who couldn't be older than twenty-five stands next to a blonde with big fake tits under her satin dress.

"Normally, this evening is about coming together to celebrate another great week on Wickett. But tonight, we decided to make our focus a little different."

They both bow their heads and paste a fake expression of remorse on their features.

"We've lost one of our own children to a tragic illness that seems nearly unstoppable.

Tyler Henry had his whole life ahead of him when his drug addiction claimed his life and shattered our community."

The room is somber and silent as they watch a slide-show of Tyler play in the background. My hands shake, so I clench my fists and bite down to stop myself from interjecting.

"His parents couldn't be with us tonight, but we'd like to make this announcement. Until now, Wickett was our home, our community, but this year it feels as if our community is sick, stricken with disease that we can't cure. That is why we've partnered with the local police force to instate a new initiative on Wickett that will eradicate the spread of drugs and crime in our precious town."

The woman beside him pipes up. "It's time to clean up our precious beach town and keep it safe for our children. No more out of control parties, illegal alcohol sales, and lethal drugs distributed on our watch. Every seedy establishment, every tattoo shop and hole-in-the-wall bar will be cleaned up or shut down."

"What!" My mouth barks before I can stop myself. All eyes in the room are on me as my breathing picks up and my heart hammers in my chest. "Tattoo shops are not the problem! Rich kids with no consequences, entitled jerks who think they take what they want—or who they want—that's the problem." I try to step forward, but I feel myself being dragged from the room. My dad's scowl fills my vision as we pass the doorway until we're in the next room.

"What is wrong with you?" he barks.

"The problem on Wickett isn't the tattoo shops and bars! Those are honest businesses that don't deserve to be shut down by some rich assholes with a grudge."

"Watch your mouth, young lady! This is a benefit for a young man."

"That young man tried to rape me!" I shout, not caring who hears me, which is likely everyone in the party since the door is only barely closed, and it's still silent on the other side.

"Sierra!" my mother gasps, her eyes wide and her face pale as she stares at me. For a moment, my heart stops, realizing that she may have finally realized the severity of this situation.

"You can't just go around making accusations like that," she whispers. It feels like I've been slapped.

"Accusations?" I mumble, tears pooling in my eyes. "He wasn't a victim of addiction. He was an asshole, and he attacked me. He was high and drunk—"

"Exactly," my dad interrupts me.

"And where were you?" my mother adds. "You put yourself in those situations, Sierra. What do you expect is going to happen?"

I can't speak. I can hardly breathe. It feels as if I'm dreaming this. They can't be serious. The next words that come out of my mouth are the thoughts that are running through my head, meant for myself. I don't care about convincing my parents anymore. "Logan saved me. He was at that party, and he didn't touch me. Not then. Not without my consent."

"Who's Logan?" my father booms, as if that's what he really needs to worry about.

"He has far more integrity than Tyler could ever have. And he doesn't deserve what these people will do to him."

"Is that the boy you've been seen with? Logan, the drug dealer?" Her face is in mine now, whisper-shouting through gritted teeth. But my mind can't get over the fact that she just said his name. It sounded so wrong on her lips.

"What about Hale?" my father adds, but I can't possibly react to that name at the moment. I let out a huff and turn away.

"I don't belong here," I whisper. The door to the next room, full of those superficial people with their fake concern and empty gestures, is cracked just enough to hear every word. So I push the heavy wood so that it flies open when I shout, "I don't want to belong here! If anyone here cared about Wickett at all, they'd leave!"

Then, I spin on my heels to make my exit when the harsh sting of a slap across my face stops me in my tracks. My mother is staring at me, her nostrils flaring. A tear falls across my cheek as I reach up to touch the burning skin of my face.

I can't say another word. Everything I want to say to them demands to be screamed, and I don't have the desire or energy to stay in this place for one more second.

So, I rush past her and out the door.

Chapter Eighteen

SIERRA

The walk from the country club to the main drag, where Logan's apartment sits above the tattoo shop, is eerily quiet. I could have ordered a ride or headed to the condo, but something pulls me toward his place, a siren song calling me home. I'm nearly there when the nightly spring rains over Wickett open up and drench me to the bone.

I knock quietly on his apartment door. My hands won't stop shaking, and my bare feet ache from running after ditching my heels back by the country club. For a moment, I'm afraid he'll be angry with me for showing up so late, but I don't have to wonder for long.

The door flies open like he's been waiting for me. There is remorse in his eyes, pain in the deep circles that cast shadows on his perfect features. He's suffered tonight—without me. And by the way he's looking at me right now, he needed me to come. He knew I would come.

He stares at my lips and then at the wet fabric that hangs over my breasts.

I don't bother to speak, and within the next breath, he's pulling me toward him, one hand looped around my waist. Our mouths crash together, and his tongue is hungry in its search for mine. He dominates my body as I gasp against his lips, claiming me, and I pray he doesn't stop this time. Tonight I don't want restraint. Tonight calls for abandon.

My soaked body comes alive as he presses his hips against mine. I can immediately feel the hard, intense pressure of his arousal against my belly, and it makes me ache in a new and thrilling way.

I do this to him, my body says. This is for me.

We stumble into his apartment and shut the door behind us. Suddenly, my back is against the hardwood, and I'm spreading my legs to make room for him, desperately hoping he fills the void.

My moan hums against his lips as he presses his body harder, grinding a rhythm I match with my own thrusts until I feel myself growing closer and closer to that sweet release I ache for. And we haven't even taken our clothes off yet. This is the constant electricity I feel around Logan, like I always have a head start to ecstasy.

I nearly whisper to him to never stop. Before I can beg him, I feel his hands move for the hem of my dress. Yes. Please, God. I want to cry out as his hand snakes up my thigh until he's gripping my bare ass in his hands.

I tear at his shirt, pulling it off in a rush so I can feel the skin of his body against my hands. He gasps against my lips as my fingers trace under the elastic of his athletic shorts. How easy it would be to just pull them away...

When he doesn't stop me with his next breath, I take it as an invitation.

Pulling the band of his shorts away from his body, I glide them down, over his massive erection, and let them drop to the floor.

He's fighting the urge to stop what's about to happen. I can feel it. So before he can, I drop to my knees before him, holding his hips in my hands.

His hungry eyes watch me as I wrap my fingers around his hardness. It's so much smoother than I expected, and I can feel my arms shaking with nerves as I slowly begin to pump from the base to the head. Logan's head falls back as his eyes roll with pleasure.

Heat pools in my belly as I watch the way my movement pleases him. His hips start to rock toward me as I continue moving back and forth until I stop. Pulling him closer, I lay a desperate kiss against his stomach, his hips, then to the base of this powerful, beautiful thing in my hands.

He groans again, pumping forward out of needy reflex.

Something takes over as I run my tongue along his length from bottom to top. Then I pull all of him into my mouth, feeling him grace the back of my throat.

"Fuck, Sierra," he growls as I start to move, stroking him at the same time.

His hands grip my hair. He seems to be restraining himself, and I'm torn between wanting him to save his orgasm for me—all of me—and wanting to feel him spend himself in my mouth, sent over this cliff of pleasure by my actions alone.

I have never felt more sexual in my life, and it's a power that I'm suddenly desperate for.

Before I get to think about it another moment, he pulls himself away. I want to cry out. This can't end now.

But he's not stopping. He's lifting me off the floor and carrying me to the bed.

"I'll never come before you," he growls as he tosses me onto my back, my dress riding up to my hips exposing myself to him. He seems to stop in mid-thought as he sees my bare sex on his bed, ready and waiting.

"Where is your underwear?" he asks.

"I wasn't wearing any."

"Sierra," he whispers as rests his hand against my knee, touching me softly. "We had a deal."

"I don't care about that deal, Logan. I want you."

He is at war with his demons. He thinks I'm something I'm not and that he has to protect me—from himself. He's awoken something in me, and I'm not going down without a fight. The damage he's doing to himself is far worse than what he could ever do to me, and I'm done letting him do this to himself.

I grab his hand from my knee and pull him closer until

he's resting between my knees. "Logan," I whimper. "I need you." Then I writhe under him so he can see the pain he's causing me.

His mouth crashes against mine. Suddenly his hardness is grinding against my core. And I'm grinding against him as he tries to peel my dress off, releasing my breasts. Immediately his mouth takes one between his lips, and I gasp. As his mouth works my nipple, he continues grinding, and I'm getting closer and closer. He knows exactly where to move because the pressure against my clit sends me flying.

Suddenly my thighs are squeezing his hips and twisting as my body convulses and my eyes roll back. I'm locked in pleasure, consumed by the raw sensation of him, and at that moment, the only thing he's fucking me with are his eyes. I never want to find pleasure without his gaze on me ever again.

"Fuck, that's the most beautiful thing I've ever seen" he says as he pulls away.

"Where are you going?" I cry, reaching for him.

"Getting my rubbers," he answers as he pulls a packet out of his nightstand drawer. I peel off the rest of my dress as he readies himself with the condom. Watching him perch over me, I can't help but admire how pains-takingly beautiful this man is. So tortured and loving with his rock-hard body and watercolor skin, I realize as I wait for him that I never want to be in this place with any other person for the rest of my life. Logan is it for me.

"Are you sure about this?" he asks as he positions himself against my entrance. In response, I wrap my legs around him and squeeze him closer. He links his fingers with mine as he lays on top of me, burning me to ash with that lustful stare. Then he takes my mouth, softly then hungrily.

He enters me slowly at first, then comes slamming in, past a short second of pain until the only sensation I know is fullness, and I never want to be without it. I let out a long, soft moan as he pulls out and slams in again. It's like I had been waiting my whole life for this. With my hands gripped tightly in his, he stares down at me as his thrusts begin to slowly pick up speed.

"Sierra," he growls against my lips like he's begging me for mercy. He slams into me, the pleasure something different, but still as intense and profound.

"Logan," I cry out in return. He and I are the only ones that exist at this very moment. The world resides in this connection between us. The contact of our bodies, intertwined and bonded, overwhelms my senses, and I'm lost in desire. He thrusts fiercely, his grunts making me wild with need for him.

"Hold on to me, baby," he whispers as he puts my arms around his neck. I do as he says, and something savage takes over as he lays his body on mine, looping one arm under my knee so his length grinds against my pleasure spot, sending me into another earth-shattering orgasm. I scream out his name as we crash as one.

After we collapse, I wrap myself in his arms, pulling his face close to mine so I can kiss him, taste him, have him forever. There will never come a time in my life when

I won't want him. I love him more than I thought possible. Especially now.

Outside, the rains continue. For a while, the sound of the drops on the roof are the only sound in the room, aside from our heavy breathing, which slows and falls into the cadence of sleep.

LOGAN

I wake to the sound of the bed creaking and the cold empty space between my arms. When I peel my eyes open, the room is still dim, but early sunlight paints the window a light blue instead of the night's pitch-black.

Sierra is sitting on the bed, facing away from me. My mind races back to what we did last night, and I feel instantly sick with regret. Her beautiful blonde hair cascades down her bare back, and I touch her lightly, hoping she's not hurting. I've never taken a girl's virginity before, so I have no clue how badly she could be feeling.

Her skin erupts in goosebumps as my fingers glide down her spine. She turns toward me, peeking over her shoulder and nailing me with a sexy smile.

"Are you okay?" I ask, leaning on my elbow.

The soft curve of her breasts silhouetted against the morning light steals my attention as she turns her body toward mine and leans forward.

"I'm perfect," she whispers. My hand grazes her rib

cage and brushes her stomach as she crawls into my arms.

"Are you trying to leave?" I ask, my lips against her hair.

"Never." Her arms squeeze around me until my body is almost completely covering hers. And the words hit me square in the gut. I don't want this girl to leave me. Ever. Even in just the last few days, I've gotten used to the idea of having her around. Having her in my tiny, shitty apartment. Cooking her meals and wrapping myself around her every night. It would be pure fucking bliss, and I'm an idiot for even considering it.

"Logan," she moans against my neck as her legs wrap around my hips. The message is pretty clear when I feel her rubbing herself against me, like she's searching for me.

"You're not still sore?" I ask. Her sex finds its mark a moment later and she nearly mounts herself on me before I can pull back. That answers my question. "Condom, baby."

I plant a kiss on her nose before reaching across the bed for the nightstand.

After I have it wrapped up, my dick buries itself inside of her and it feels like falling into a warm slice of heaven. We move slowly against each other, her moaning and writhing beneath me like she was made to find this pleasure.

Her hair is fanned out around her head now, a halo for the angel I don't deserve. As I let my ink-stained hands grace the skin of her body, I worship every inch. She clings to my shoulders, waiting for me to bring the force like last night, but I'm too lost in this slow love-making to rail into her like I did before. Like I should not have done. I got lost with need last night. Now, I promise to be easier on her.

She pulls my face down for a kiss, and a grunt escapes my lips as her legs squeeze my hips tighter. Our foreheads touch, our heavy breaths meeting in the space between our lips.

When I feel her pulsing with pleasure, I watch her face as the ecstasy rolls through her. It's so fucking exquisite that it slams me headfirst into my orgasm.

"I love you," she says against my mouth as I lose the strength to hold my body above hers and crash safely between her legs.

My mind reels from her words. It's ridiculous and impossible. She can't love me. Not me, and not after only one week.

But it doesn't change the fact that I feel the same way. I love her in a way that is dangerous and fucking mind-blowing. I love her in the same way sirens pull men to their deaths. I know it will kill me, but I don't care. I would gladly give my life to whisper those words back to her.

"I love you so fucking much."

My nerves are on edge. In two hours, I'll be handing the money over to Hale and will be officially done with his bullshit. I'll be free. To what? I don't know. Sierra tells me what her parents did to her last night, and I'm sick. No fucking way my girl deserves to be treated like that. It takes everything in me not to go over there myself and give those fucks a piece of my mind. But she made me promise. And I'll never break a promise to her.

Neither of us want to leave this apartment. Today is officially Sierra's last day on Wickett. Once I get this drop-off taken care of, she has to go. The air in the apartment is tense and just fucking sad. I can't take my hands off of her body, like if I let her go for one second, she'll disappear.

I don't know if the fact that we used up the rest of my condoms after breakfast makes it better or worse.

Before we know it, it's time to meet Hale. She stares at me, teary-eyed from the bed as I put on my leather jacket. I can see the goodbye on her lips, and it's fucking crushing me.

"Logan," she breathes. "About the drop-off..."

"I'll be fine," I say, but I can't promise it's true. Hale could have who-knows-what up his sleeve and to be totally fucking honest, I'm nervous. But I can't tell her that.

"I have to go." Her voice is so small from the bed, curled up in the shirt and skirt she wore over here last night.

Her words sting. I know she'll go. Not just to her parents, but back to her life. The beautiful, scarless pure life she lives in Newport. It stings that she doesn't want to see this part. The end. Or is it the beginning?

"Logan, I have to go to the drop-off."

"No, baby." I walk up to her and place my hands over

her cheeks. "You can't be there. Who the fuck knows what's going to go down? I can't put you in danger."

A tear rolls down her cheek and she shuts her eyes like I've caused her pain. "No, Logan. He said I have to be the one to do the drop-off."

I feel the blood drain from my cheeks. Her words beat through my skull like a drum. Of course, he's taunting me. Of course, he wants me to give him everything. One more knot in the noose.

"Not an option," I croak, but it feels weak.

"It's the only option. He won't meet you. It has to be me." She presses up on her knees so her face is closer to mine, but I step away. I can't let her feel my hands shaking.

"Why didn't you tell me?" I don't mean for it to sound so accusatory, but it hurts to know she held this information alone. The fear she must have felt all night, knowing what she was up against today. And all I could think about was getting my dick wet.

Fuck. Freedom was so close, and now it's farther than it's ever been because I'll drop Hale's dead body in the ocean before I let him bring Sierra into this again.

"I'm sorry," she sobs as she reaches for me, but I can't let her touch me. I'm poison.

Turning away from her drives a rage through me, and I turn and hammer my fist into the wall, feeling the skin break and the bones rattle. Sierra screams.

The pain does nothing to distract me, but it clears my mind. I should have never let it get this far, never should have given in to the temptation. And if I really loved her at all, I'd make sure she'd never trust me again.

"Get out," I growl, keeping my face away from her.

She sobs out and runs her nails across the skin of my back. "Logan, I'm not scared. I can do this."

"This is my business," I bark at her. The pain from hurling my anger at her hurts me more than it could hurt her. "You had no right to get involved. Did you ever think that he's using you to nail me?"

"No," she cries through her trembling lips. "It's not like that."

"What do you know?" When I step up to her, my voice booming, she flinches. And I splinter into a million pieces, too broken to ever be repaired again. But I've already gotten this far, it couldn't get any worse now...

"You don't know a fucking thing, princess. I didn't have the heart to tell you before, Sierra, but you're the fucking reason I lost that stash in the first place. I was too busy babysitting you the night of the bonfire when I had other shit to do."

Her face shows a glimpse of anger, which is good. Get angry, baby.

"You come around here once a year to get some grungy local to stick his hands down your pants and now you think you know what it's like. You don't belong here, you can't stay here, and now that I've gotten a taste, you're nothing but a pain in my fucking ass now."

Tears are streaming violently down her face. Her expression reeks of fear. I need her to hurt, enough to make her leave. To get back in her parents' perfect Mercedes and drive all the way back to Newport. She'll cry, hate me, swear off Wickett forever, and move on with her life. Without me, but safe.

"Now, get the fuck out while I figure out what the hell I'm going to do."

I don't expect the slap, but I should. I know Sierra enough now to realize that she doesn't take shit from anybody, least of all from some scumbag like me.

Her hand stings against my cheek, and it really does hurt. And I'm glad it hurts. I want it to hurt. I wish she could carve my heart out of my chest.

"You're a fucking coward," she bites, standing up to me like she could take me.

Then, she spins on her heels and runs out the front door with nothing but her purse and jacket in her hands.

I stand in my studio apartment without moving for at least five full minutes. The only sound is the blood dripping from my busted hand onto the cheap floor. Then I realize that I was supposed to meet Hale fifteen minutes ago, and no matter what happened with Sierra, I need this dickhead off my back. If I don't show at all, he's more likely to go after her, and he knows enough about her family and parents to find her.

So I reach for the folded envelope with the cash from the bike. I left it on the table by the door this morning so I wouldn't forget it when it's time to go. But the table by the door is empty as fuck. After a rushed search of my apartment, I let my mind accept what I already know to be true. Sierra took the cash.

Chapter Nineteen

SIERRA

I sit in the diner bathroom for at least fifteen minutes before I'm able to come out without tears streaming down my face. I know what Logan is doing. It's obvious. He's trying to keep me safe and is pushing me away. I'm mostly just upset that he wouldn't trust me. He should have known that I wouldn't leave him and he doesn't have to leave me. We're in this together.

He lashed out to break my heart and drive me away, and honestly, I'm still fuming about it. But first, I need to take care of this Hale situation. He's been blowing up my phone for almost an hour. I answer him back: on my way.

If I didn't take the money, then Logan would have gone, and if he went to the drop-off, then the whole thing would be ruined. Right now, my only goal is to get him free of Hale's hold, and then we can focus on us.

We agreed to meet at the gazebo. It's quiet. Most vacationers are leaving today, and it's overcast and chillier than normal anyway. So when I walk up to the center of the giant round structure, it's just me, and once I make out his form, Hale. He's looking impatient as he scrolls through his phone.

"I don't like to wait."

"You'll live," I answer.

"Where's your boyfriend?"

"You told me to come alone." My voice is cold and empty, much like how I feel.

"You look like you've been crying. I take it he wasn't too excited about you coming alone. Honestly, I'm surprised he let his girlfriend do his dirty work."

"What now?" I ask, feeling more and more impatient.

"Now you give me the cash."

I pull the envelope out of my purse, my hand shaking. It's almost over, I tell myself. I just hand it over, and everything is done.

"This is everything you made?" he asks, and I feel my blood go cold.

"This is exactly what we owe you," I answer with a harsh stare.

"I gave you a kilo to sell."

I don't answer. Red flags are going off in my head. I

need to do something, say something, but I can't process what is real and what is not real. I just want him to take the money. So, I nod.

"And this is the ten G's from what you sold? Of the Wicked mix?"

"Why do you keep asking me that?" I bark back at him. "You know exactly what this money is for. We owe you ten thousand, so here it is."

He laughs. "Okay." He's toying with me, and my skin feels on edge as I stare at him. Like the gazebo is getting bigger and smaller at the same time.

Quickly, I shove the envelope in his hands and turn to walk away. Behind me, he's still laughing. Nausea rolls through me like getting toppled over by a large wave in the sea.

"Freeze," a harsh voice barks from the side of the gazebo.

My heart hammers in my chest. And for a moment, I tell myself that I have nothing to worry about. I'm innocent, just dropping off some money that was owed to a friend.

But I know better.

As the man in black walks toward me, I realize that he doesn't have a gun pointed at me, but he does have his hand ready like a cowboy during a shoot-out. I stop dead in my tracks and put my hands up slowly. I can see his badge now, hanging on his hip.

And when I look up into his eyes, I realize that I'm not who he was expecting. He's a good-looking man, in a black shirt and pants with shoulders as broad as Logan's and tattoos peeking out from his short sleeves. His forehead creases when my eyes meet his. And we share a moment. I don't know if he's pleading with me or I'm pleading with him.

From the other side of the gazebo, another cop in uniform ambushes me. He grabs my arm abruptly and twists it behind my back.

The young cop in black barks at him. "Easy! She's not resisting."

Before I can blink, my hands are in cuffs and tears are pooling in my eyes.

Then, just as I watch him swallow with a face of remorse, the broad-shouldered cop reads me my rights.

LOGAN

By the time I get to the pier, they're already gone. There is only one patrol car left, but I don't know the cop and he won't give me any information, no matter how aggressively I demand it.

There's one person I can call, and I'm desperately hoping he can help me.

As I jog back to the shop, hoping Murph will be there to lend me his car so I can get to the station, I dial up Rafe on my phone.

He doesn't answer on the first dial. Bullshit.

I dial again.

"I'm a little busy right now," Rafe growls on the other

end of the line.

"Don't you fucking dare book her. It's me you want," I bark as I yank open the door of the shop.

"I can't do this right now."

The line goes dead. That asshole.

Murph is standing behind the counter and takes one look at me.

"I need to borrow your car."

"Tell me what happened first," he demands.

"I can't." Which is true. I can't speak about this, not yet. Not until I get her out of this mess. Because if I speak about it, then that makes it true. Sierra is in fucking jail—because of me. She should be packing up to head home after another harmless week spent at Wickett, but instead, she's in jail. For me.

"Please," I growl through my teeth. My body is a live wire, ready to snap if I don't fix this now.

He keeps his brow furrowed and his eyes on me as he pulls his keys from his pocket and tosses them in my direction.

"You know if you need backup…" he says, but I don't stay for the end of that statement. I don't need to. I already know.

I pull up to the station a moment later. Wickett Beach Police Station is small and only fully staffed during this week of the year. So the first thing I see when I fly through the front doors is Rafe standing behind the counter and Sierra in the back of the room, her hands in cuffs and her head hanging.

Rafe looks up at me with a scowl. "Don't make a scene," he demands.

He rounds the counter before I can barge through the door to the back of the room. His hands land squarely against my chest as he pushes me toward the exit.

"Let's go have a chat," he orders.

I let him push me toward his office, but only after my eyes lock with Sierra's. She is miserable, terrified, and behind all of that is a layer of pissed off.

So am I.

It doesn't take a genius to figure out Hale double-crossed us. He must have traded Sierra's freedom for his immunity.

Rafe's office is small, and the two of us barely fit in there together, but that doesn't seem to matter much because he is in my face.

"I promised your brother, along with Murph, that we would look after you, and today, I thought I failed him. One of my guys picked up that little pompous rich asshole for dealing a couple days ago, and what do you think he did? He started spilling names like the credits rolling after a fucking movie. I bet you can guess whose name was the first on his lips."

"Then book me," I growl, stepping up to him.

"I can't, Logan. Because the only person I have any proof on is her. You wanna tell me why the fuck I have this girl in custody right now? Because this is about to be a goddamn nightmare for me. You know that, right?"

"Then let her go."

He runs his hands through his hair and turns away. If

he thinks I'm getting on his nerves now, he has no idea how bad I can make things for him if he doesn't help me fix this.

"It's not that easy, Logan. God dammit! I asked you to stay out of trouble, but you didn't, did you? You've been using, dealing, and bringing the trust fund girls into it. I'll have the mayor on the line any minute chewing my ass out."

"You told me to stay out of trouble? That's really easy for you, Rafe, when you can just disappear after Theo died!" Rage and anger course through my veins. The guy I thought I could trust more than my own brother looks like a stranger to me now.

"How could I target anyone on Wickett if they knew our connection? The second you started selling, you fucked yourself, Logan. I've been trying to clean up this city since Theo died because I never wanted what happened to him to happen to anyone else. But you, you fucked everything."

I don't speak as his words run their course through my mind. The reason Rafe stopped coming around was because of me. Not exactly the news I want to process right now, but it's definitely something I'll have to come back to later.

He takes a deep breath and braces his hands on his desk. "You and I know exactly how this is going to go down. We watched those rich fucks do it all of our lives while the rest of us suffered the consequences. Her parents will make a call, drop some cash, maybe buy some updated parking meters for the north lot, and Sierra's record will dissolve like someone just dropped it into the ocean."

He lays a hand on my shoulder and gives me a tight squeeze. "You marching in here, making a scene and trying to solve this on your own will only cause more problems."

Something in me crumbles. He's right, and I could punch a hole straight through the station with all of my pent-up anger. It should be me saving her, making this right. I should be the knight that takes her away from this mess, but then I remember the way I treated her this morning. Kicking her while she was down just to keep her out of it.

A lot of fucking good that did.

"Promise me you won't put her in the cell. Promise me you'll keep her comfortable until her parents show up."

"I promise."

I look at Rafe, a face I haven't really looked at in over a year. It reminds me too much of my brother. They ran together with Murph since I was in diapers, and occasionally once I was older, they let me tag along. Now I was all that was left of him, and the pain is too much for either of us to handle, so I turn away and stalk out to the lobby.

When I look back at Sierra, she keeps her eyes trained forward. She won't look at me, and rightfully so. I am a piece of shit, and I don't deserve to lick the floor she steps on.

"Get her out of the goddamn cuffs," I gripe when Rafe meets me in the lobby.

"I will," he says, clapping a hand on my shoulder again. Then, he stands between me and her while I walk out the front door. She never looks up, not even once.

Chapter Twenty

SIERRA

My parents don't even come to pick me up at the jail. They send a lawyer. The paperwork is minimal, and the nice good-looking cop lets me keep my phone and gives me a cup of coffee while I wait.

I have a feeling he isn't any happier about my being here than I am.

Before my lawyer shows up, he takes me back to the interrogation room, and his weathered expression tells me that his little visit with Logan took a toll. I don't know who this man is, but it's clear he knows Logan. I can only assume it's due to Logan's troubled past, but maybe there is more. They look close enough in age, so it's possible they're friends.

"You don't need to talk. You can wait for your lawyer," he says as he places a paper cup on the table.

"I'll tell you whatever you want."

I heard what he said to Logan. My parents will pay the chief of police or mayor or someone, and this will get dropped. I'll never appear in court or have anything on my record, which makes me more sick than relieved. Logan would have faced a far worse fate for no good reason at all.

"Did you sell drugs on Wickett?"

"No," I answer bluntly.

"Why were you giving Hale money?"

"Someone I care about owed him money."

"For what?"

"Drugs," I answer. He grimaces. This numb confidence has me feeling more tired than scared. I don't care what he thinks, but if he expects that I'll drop Logan's name, he's crazy.

"What's your friend's name?" he asks, but the look on his face says that he knows I won't spill, but it's worth a try.

"Not a chance."

He nods his head.

"If it makes any difference, my friend didn't sell them. They were stolen."

"Really?" he asks with sudden interest. "You know, if this goes to court, you'll have to give up some names, or it'll be you who does the time."

I don't react. That won't happen. We both know it.

A moment later, a familiar man in a tight suit walks in. "Let's go, Ms. Pearson."

I stare at the young cop, whose shoulders sag, but his eyes never leave mine.

"I lost a good friend to drug addiction," he says, and suddenly it all makes sense. He was a friend of Logan's brother, which explains how they know each other. He's testing me, to see how well I know him. How much he's really told me.

"Then, you want the same thing I want."

"Don't say a word, Sierra," the stiff lawyer behind me barks.

"I want to get rid of whoever is dealing on my beach."

"Me too," I whisper as I stand and let the white-haired man take my arm and lead me outside to his hired car. I climb into the backseat and stay silent as the man behind the wheel drives us across town to my parents' condo.

But he misses the turn.

"Where are we going?" I ask, my cheeks flushing with heat. I already know the answer.

"Your parents asked that I deliver you to Newport." I don't even remember this emotionless man's name, but he's crushing my heart right now. I claw at the door, as if it were even able to open I would barrel out of a flying vehicle just to get back to Logan.

"No!" I shout, but he doesn't react. I want to rip that phone out of his hands.

Quickly reaching for my phone, I dial up my mom and

wait for her to answer. It doesn't take more than two rings, and she starts speaking before I even have the chance.

"You've humiliated our family, Sierra. I don't know what's gotten into you, but we can never show our faces at Wickett again, and it's all your fault."

"You can't do this to me! Leave me here," I sob.

"So you can continue dealing drugs, Sierra? You think that's the life you want?"

I can hear the emotion in her voice. She's distressed and desperate.

"I wasn't! I was just—"

"We know about him," my mother barks. "That junkie you've been...going around with."

She can't say his name. She can't even find a word in her vocabulary for our relationship.

"I love him." Tears are running down my face. When I draw my hand to my mouth, I can still smell him. His cologne, his lips, his sweat. I am infused with him, and I swear to myself, I will find a way back. If I have to hitch-hike back to Wicked, I will.

My mother takes a deep breath. "I don't even know you anymore, Sierra."

I let out a wrangled sob. "No, Mom. You never did."

I press the red end button and weep silently into my hands as the driver delivers me to my parents and away from Logan.

LOGAN

She's gone. Her parents' condo is empty. This life of mine finally scared her away. It's for the best, I keep telling myself. She's better off far away from Wickett.

But then I remember the smell of her hair and the feel of her legs wrapped around my body, and my heart lurches in my chest. For a moment, I hoped that I could lead a normal life—a happy one where I had far more than I deserved. A life that made me want to be better. A life where the only thing I was getting high on was Sierra.

That life is gone now.

But that doesn't mean I can't still make some changes for the better. As I make my way back to my apartment, I pull out my phone and open a group message that has been silent for too long.

Meet at the shop in fifteen.

They don't answer, but I can see that they read it. Whether they'll show or not, I don't know, but if they're anything like they used to be, there is nothing that will stop them from showing.

As soon as I enter my apartment, my phone pings in my pocket.

About fucking time.

Saved in my phone as RC, I smile when I read it. I had a feeling he'd be the easiest to convince.

I'm getting distracted. What I need is shoved in the back of my closet, but I have to prepare myself before I pull it out. Taking a deep breath, I flick on the light and stare at the old cardboard box hidden under the old tattoo supplies. I can smell the worn leather before I even lift the flaps, but my breath hitches in my throat when I do.

Laying folded at the top is the familiar black leather jacket that I remembered. How many times was he wearing it when he pulled me into a tight hug? Or when he slammed me against the wall for being a rebellious shithead?

The biggest question swimming around the back of my mind as I stare at it: did I even deserve to put it on?

Sierra would think so.

When I unfold the leather, my fingers run across the Wicked MC patch across the chest. I feel a laugh bubble up from my chest when I remember the day Theo had them made for him and the guys. How young they were then. All foster care kids, they found each other, desperate for a family and someone to always have each other's back. The motorcycle club idea started out as a joke. Then, it became something more.

Until he died.

Then, it ended.

My phone pings again. I stare down at a message from Murph.

Ready when you are.

He would be harder to answer to, but it was time to face the music. I have some repenting to do, and there is no better time than now.

Folding the jacket under my arm, I bolt out of the apartment and get back to the shop.

The guys are already there when I show up. The curtains of the shop are pulled closed and their eyes watch me coldly as I walk in.

Rafe stands near the door, his arms crossed. He's dressed in black almost all the time. Black T-shirt, nearly black jeans. The gun is still hanging from his hip, but he has his badge out, which is customary.

Murph is sitting on his work stool in his station. His broad shoulders are intimidating as he perches his elbows on his knees and stares up at me, waiting.

It's just the three of us for now. The other guys, Murph's other friends, would do anything Murph told them to, which means he told them to stay back for now.

Their eyes land on the black jacket under my arm as soon as I step in.

"Umm..." I mutter, unsure of how to start.

Probably best at this point to just dive right in.

"My brother was the smart one. He was the good one. I was the fuck-up. The drug addict, the lost cause. He had you guys, but honestly...I thought for a long time that if he had you, then he didn't need me."

Rafe tries to interject, but I hold my hand up. "Let me finish."

"You guys had each other's backs. And he tried to get me to join you, a lot. But I wanted to be alone. It felt easier to keep the disappointment to myself. Then, he died. And...I blamed you guys."

Murph's eyes land sharply on me.

"And I know you help me out for him."

It gets quiet for a moment, and I lose sight of what I'm trying to say. Murph stands and meets me eye-to-eye. He's a few inches taller than me, and easily the biggest of the group. His thick beard and gray patches at his temples make him the most intimidating too.

He grabs the jacket from under my arm, and I take a heavy breath, waiting to see what he'll do. I won't fight Murph. I wouldn't lay a hand on any of these guys. But I'm depending on him to hear me out and give me a chance.

Opening the jacket, his fingers run along the patch the same way mine did.

"We did fail Theo," he mumbles. "If I had known about his addiction, I would have stopped it. And in that sense, we failed you too."

He holds the jacket out for me to take.

"Now we can either keep blaming each other for the shit we didn't do, or we can start acting like brothers and take care of each other so it doesn't happen again."

I take the jacket and slide my arms in, reveling in the near perfect fit. Theo was only a little shorter than me, but he was equally as broad.

"This town has gone to shit," Rafe pipes in from his stance by the counter. "I'm sick of cleaning up these little rich fuckers' messes.

"Lucky for us, I know exactly who to blame," I say to Rafe.

"So do I," he answers.

Chapter Twenty-One

SIERRA
One month later

Days are crawling by. After my parents brought me back, I could feel my mother trying to repair her relationship with me, but I've completely closed myself off. They suspected I was on drugs for the first week because I rarely came out of my room. Logan ignored all of my texts, and the idea that he really was just using me for sex became less and less impossible. I refuse to believe that it's anything less than him trying to protect me.

In fact, it seems everyone is trying to protect me. Without any contribution from me.

After the first week of mostly crying and refusing to eat or see anyone, I thought about Mrs. Walker. I wished I could be back in the bookstore, arranging new releases and hosting events. I realized that more than anything, that's what I wanted. So I applied for a business degree program to my mother's extreme excitement. It was online, but it was something. They tried to talk me into a university residency, but I couldn't bear the thought of laying down a foundation anywhere but Wicked.

My parents would never let me go back, not with my trust fund money, which they still controlled until I finish college. So, I am stuck dreaming about the bookstore that will eventually be mine, and try as hard as I can not to dream about the man who I thought would be mine.

Coming back from a hot yoga class, I keep my eyes glued on my phone as I waltz in the front door. My face is still beet red, and my legs feel like Jell-O, but I can sense something is up when I find the front door open just a crack.

Assuming it's just my mom home early from her shopping trip, I step into the living room and glance up from my phone. A clipped scream bolts out of my chest when my gaze lands on a man standing in the back corner of the living room.

His face is bulging with purple and black swelling around his lips and eyes, but the quaffed blond locks and familiar stance catches me off guard.

Hale.

"No," I whisper. Glancing around, I realize that we're

alone. We're alone, and he's pointing a gun directly at me.

I want to pass out. The room sways and a bout of tunnel vision has me staggering, but I grip the back of the couch in my hand and wait. Questions swirl around in my mind. Is he here to steal from us? Kidnap me? Hurt me?

But most of all...who did this to his face?

I have a slight suspicion that refuses to be acknowledged. If Logan did this...then he's fallen farther down than before.

"How did you get in here?" I ask, my voice shaking.

"You don't think I grew up in a house just like this one? It takes one to know one, Sierra. You only set the alarm during the night. The door lock code is a birth year. These security measures only make you feel comfortable, but they don't really protect you, do they?"

"What happened to your—"

"Your fucking boyfriend!" he barks at me, spit flying out of his swollen lips. "And he's going to pay. He'll pay for everything, then I swear to God, I'll kill him."

Tears prick my eyes when his words hit me like knives. He wants to hurt Logan, and he won't hesitate hurting me to do it.

"What—"

"You're going to walk out front and get in the car. Do you understand me? You won't fight or run, and if you do, I swear I'll shoot you in the street. I don't give a fuck anymore."

I believe him. He has a maniacal, desperate look in his

eye which terrifies me to the point of feeling entirely numb to the barrel of the gun still aimed directly at me.

"Okay," I answer with my hands up.

And I do what he says. We walk outside, him right on my tail as I get into his Volvo. He grabs my phone and turns it off before tossing it into the backseat so that I'm stuck with him in painful, terrified silence for the two-hour drive back to the beach.

LOGAN

Business has been slow lately. Spring break is over, and until summer officially kicks off, we try to enjoy the silence. But for some reason, my nerves are on edge today. And not from a jonesing sort of anxiety either. I don't get that so much anymore. This is more of an uneasy feeling, like I want to pull out my phone and call Sierra just to hear her voice.

Although I wouldn't dare. She left Wickett a month ago and hasn't looked back since. Wherever she is now, she's probably doing just fine without me. Better than being in jail at least—where she was last time I saw her. A vision I would never get out of my mind as long as I lived.

Murph stepped out to take care of some city council shit for the shop, so I'm manning this slow Thursday night business alone. I just finished a sleeve I'd been working on since last summer, and the rest of the schedule is empty.

I have all the stations cleaned and supplies put away when I hear a car door slam shut in the alley behind the shop. Cars rarely park back there so I feel immediately uneasy with the sound.

A moment later, I hear the muffled sound of voices outside the door. Then, a knock. A soft knock.

"Logan," she mumbles in a tone that makes the blood in my veins turn frigid. She's upset or terrified, and I'm across the room and pulling open the door before I can take my next breath.

I just want to see her face. Breathe the same air. Hold her, touch her.

But the sight I'm met with does not give me the pleasure I crave. The first thing I notice is the apologetic expression on her face, her tear-soaked eyes, and the tremble in her hands.

The second thing I notice is the hand gripped around her waist, pulling her against a body that isn't mine. The face attached to that body is purple and swollen from a very recent beating.

A beating I did not do.

My fists clench, and I let out a snarl as Hale's blood-red eyes meet my face. He grimaces at me like he needed an innocent girl as a shield just to face me. My innocent girl.

He doesn't let me get a word in before he flashes the gun at me then jams it back into Sierra's spine. She winces when he does, and I want to kill him so bad at that moment that it scares even me. I've never wanted to truly kill someone before, but right now, I would find no greater joy in the world than watching this piece of scum suffer in a slow, painful death.

"Let her go," I growl.

"Not a fucking chance," he snaps back. "You stole my shit!"

I put my hands up toward him because I can see him losing it. He's erratic, too erratic for my comfort while he's got that weapon on her. All I can think is how I'm going to get that thing off her, even if it means putting it on me.

"I don't know what you're talking about," I say gently, careful not to rile him up.

"The fuck you don't. You took my supply, twice now, you piece of shit! The whole fucking stock!" He's shaking, and Sierra has her eyes clenched shut in fear. How the fuck have I gotten her back into this shit? I wanted her safe and gone from my life, but this dick dragged her right back. And for that he will pay.

"Why would I take your stock? I don't sell anymore. Ask anyone."

"You must think I'm so stupid," Hale spits back at me. "You did it as payback, you piece of fucking white trash. You're not smarter than me. You stole my supply, and now they're on my ass, and because of you, they did this shit to my fucking face!" He motions to the swelling around his lips and eyes, and I grit my teeth together to stop myself from fighting with him.

I didn't take his supply, but I know what he's referring to. When I lost my stash back during spring break with

Sierra, he was the one who stole it from me. Rafe helped me figure it out. He clued me in on the tracking app Hale had embedded onto my phone as a means of keeping tabs on me. When I ditched the bonfire that night—the bonfire I was supposed to be selling at—Hale found me and did one better. Framed me for losing his supply and made me pay it back with the sale of my bike.

"Why don't you put down the gun?" I suggest gently. I need to keep him busy at this point and buy us time.

"Fuck you!" He snaps, jabbing the gun tighter against her back. Her eyes widen in terror.

"What do you want me to do?" I yell back. We're hidden in the narrow alley by his car on one side and a pair of dumpsters on the other.

"I want you to get these assholes off my back!" He glances around like he expects them to be watching him.

"I'll help you. I promise. Just let her go. You don't need her anymore." I step closer and in response, he steps back again.

"The fuck you will!"

I catch movement in the corner of my eye, but I do my best not to react to it. There's no way I'm going to fuck this up now. This is my last chance to make it right for Sierra, and I'm not about to let her down.

Chapter Twenty-Two

SIERRA

Something about Logan gives me hope. In the car, I had to consider that this was it. I was going to die at the hands of a power-hungry maniac with a gun. Someone who doesn't like being humiliated or outsmarted.

"You're going to call them. From my phone," Hale barks as he tosses Logan the cellphone with his free hand. "Call them now and tell them you have their goods. Do it now!"

The barrel presses into my spine, and all I keep thinking is that he's squeezing it so hard his finger could slip, and I'd be gone before I even hit the ground.

"Okay, okay!" Logan answers as he turns on the phone.

Hale tells him the number to dial as Logan's hands shake.

"Don't do it, Logan!" The words slip out of my mouth before I can stop them. I can't let Logan get back into this mess. He's already been clean for so long, and if he calls those guys, they will either force him back into the business or they will kill him. Either way, the Logan I love is gone.

He looks up at my face, and there's a hint of something in his eyes that squeezes my heart until a tear slides across my cheek. It's a look that asks me to trust him. A knowing look that quiets me.

"No," I whisper.

"Shut. Up." Hale snarls against my cheek. "Make the call!"

"What makes you think they'll believe me?"

"Because you're going to be very convincing," he snaps as his hand wraps around my throat. He squeezes, and I can immediately feel my pulse slow.

Suddenly, there's a noise at the end of the alleyway. It sounds like a shoe scraping against the gravel, and Hale turns his head for a split second, long enough for Logan to pounce.

"Freeze!" a familiar voice barks from far away.

Logan's hand is around my waist as I'm hoisted over his body and to the ground. There's a struggle. I turn in time to see Hale throw a punch at Logan's jaw, but he dodges it and dives for the gun in Hale's hand. They fight for a moment before I spot Rafe, the young cop jumping over the hood of the car to help Logan force Hale to the ground.

Somewhere in the struggle, Logan loses his grip on Hale, and all I hear is the deafening sound of the gunshot.

"Logan!" My voice aches with the scream as I watch wide-eyed to see Logan staring down at his body. Then he looks up at Hale and throws a punch so hard against his jaw that he passes out cold on the cement.

I jump from my place on the ground and throw myself into Logan's arms.

"Oh my God, are you hurt?" I scream against the skin of his neck. I don't have the guts to look for myself. I just need to feel his body close to mine, his voice in my ear, his breath on my skin.

"I'm fine," he answers as he squeezes me tighter. "It was just a graze. Are you okay?"

He pulls me away and looks at my body as if I have some sort of hidden bullet wound. "I'm fine," I echo as I pull him back in for another hug. I still don't know if he's going to push me away after today, so I'm going to get as much of this nearness as I can.

"Do I need to call an ambulance?" Rafe asks.

Logan and I pull our bodies away and look at the cop who has Hale cuffed and leaning against the car even though he's still unconscious.

"For him, maybe," Logan answers.

"Nah. He's gonna suffer through that concussion he's got. I'm taking him in on intent to distribute.

"How did you know he was here?" Logan asks.

"Her parents called me about twenty minutes ago. Said her car was there, but she was missing. They suspected it had something to do with Wickett, and I figured he'd come here. They're on their way now."

My cheeks flush, thinking about my parents coming back to Wicked, seeing me in Logan's arms, knowing that this trouble will follow him wherever he goes. They'll never let me come back, and they'll give me hell for it as long as they can. It only makes me squeeze his waist even tighter, whether he wants me to or not.

"I knew he'd come after me eventually, but I never thought he'd bring her into this," Logan says as he squeezes my waist tighter again.

Rafe grimaces and rubs the thin layer of stubble along his chin and cheeks. Then, he glances up at something above us against the wall. "Yeah, why don't we get him into the car before we start discussing that?"

I try to see what it is he's looking at, but Logan distracts me with a look before I can see it. "I'll bring her to the station," he says to Rafe as the cop hoists a barely conscious Hale to his feet and shoves him in the back of the cop car.

"Sounds good," Rafe answers. "Sure you don't want a ride?"

"No, we need to talk." His eyes stay trained on mine as he speaks.

A chill runs down my spine.

"I'll get this towed," Rafe calls as he passes Hale's car. "Unless you want it." He smiles and winks at Logan just before he disappears into his own patrol car.

A moment later, Logan has his hand on my lower back and is leading me back into the shop. Once we're inside,

I realize how shaken I am. He runs to the back and returns with a bottle of water and a wet washcloth that he uses to wipe my face slowly like I'm a child.

"Are you sure you're okay?" he asks, unscrewing the cap of the water bottle and handing it to me. I take a long drink, not realizing how thirsty I was.

I can't speak, but the feeling of being alone with him again threatens to break me.

"I am now," I muster.

"Goddamn, Sierra. If I had any idea he would come after you..."

I stop his words with my own. There are still so many questions I need answers to. "What do you have to do with this, Logan?"

"I don't want you to worry about me," he answers.

"I'm going to decide, whether you want me to or not. Logan, I—"

His lips are against mine. It's like a fresh gasp of air, and I pull him desperately against my body. When his tongue slips past my lips, I drop the mostly empty water bottle and wrap my arms around him. He lifts me as my legs wrap around his waist.

"God, I missed this," he whispers against my mouth. He sets me on the counter and keeps his body between my legs.

I want him to tear off my clothes and let him lose himself in my body again like that first night, but I need answers. I need to know that Logan isn't lost to the seedy world I found him in.

"Don't avoid the question," I whisper, pulling back so

he can't kiss the question away.

Letting out a sigh, he realizes that I'm not going to stop asking until I know the truth. "Rafe and I have it under control. The less you know the better."

It physically hurts me to do it, but I press his body away from mine and his face falls.

"No," I snap. "I love being back here with you, but I'm not going to be silent and stupid."

"I would never..." he says, trying to touch my cheek.

"Be honest with me," I answer, pulling back again. "Are you dealing again?"

He smiles, then he lets his head fall into my lap. "No, baby. I promise you. I'm not dealing." His kisses trail up from my thighs to my arms, and it feels so good, I think I can die from it, but I manage to push him away again.

"Then what was Hale talking about?"

"You're killing me."

"I don't care," I say as strongly as I can. "Logan, if you're going to keep things from me, then I'm going to walk away right now."

"Rafe and I stole his supply. We burned every last ounce, but we knew his dealers would come after him, and we've been watching him, knowing that we'd have leverage over him. That he'd spill his supplier to keep his own ass safe."

He whispers it against my fingers, and I smile at him, not only because he's not the same broken man I met a month ago. The Logan I knew played the victim, always one step behind and second-guessing himself. This Logan is ahead of the game, methodical, and hungry for justice.

He's not holding back with his kisses anymore either. It's like he's been unleashed and letting himself show affection.

And I want it all.

LOGAN

I can't take my hands off of Sierra. Something about seeing her terrified for her life makes me want to hold her and never let her go. But the gnawing reminder that she was put in that situation because of me has me hesitating. Will she forgive me for pushing her away so cruelly? Should she?

Fuck no.

What kind of man would I be if I kept her around if it only puts her in danger?

Not the kind she deserves.

After giving her the answers she wants, explaining the new cameras installed in the alleyway to catch Hale when he would inevitably show up, I take her to the station. She tries to stall. She wants to wrap those perfect, long legs around my waist again, and I want that as much as she does, but my head keeps reminding me that I'm a piece of shit if I let her back into my life.

In Murph's car on the way to the station, I feel her watching me. I can read the questions on her face. So, I reach across the console and take her hand.

We don't speak, even though I have a thousand fucking apologies docked and waiting. But I don't have the guts to utter even one. Because once I get those out of the way, then we'll be moving on to the "what's next?" question we're both thinking about. And I know that what's next is going to break my heart...again.

Her parents are standing outside the station when I pull up. Her mother looks like she's been crying by the red patches across her pale skin. Her father looks pissed, seething with anger, his nostrils flaring and his eyes wide.

I'm not a fucking coward, but if I were, I wouldn't even bother getting out of the car. Sierra is the first one out, and her parents are on her in a flash. Her mom has her tied up in a tight hug as her father just lays a hand on her back.

When I get out, I see Rafe in the station. He gives me a head nod, and just as I'm about to head in to speak to him—and get as far away from the awkward encounter I would face with Sierra's parents—a voice booms in my direction.

"Son."

I turn to see Sierra's dad, a tall, broad man glaring at me. Great.

"Stay right there."

Her mother seems to notice me for the first time, and her face contorts in a grimace like she's about to start crying even more. Then, she's running for me. And I actually flinch. This tiny woman wants to rip my fucking face off, and I don't doubt she could.

Instead of going for my eyeballs, she wraps her little arms around my neck and pulls me down for a hug. Which is more shocking than having my eyeballs ripped out.

She's practically hugging a statue because I can't move. Then, the broad man lands a hand on my shoulder. "Detective Crawford told us what you did."

"You saved our little girl," the woman sobs into my jacket.

My shoulders settle as I lock eyes with Sierra on the other side of the car. She has a tight smile, biting her bottom lip in between her teeth.

When we go inside, Rafe puts us all in an office while he gets the report from Sierra. Her parents are adamant about pressing charges, but only until Rafe explains that it would require court time and more trauma for Sierra.

"What do you suggest?" Sierra asks with a level head.

"The information we got from him will ensure that he faces a good amount of jail time. Going against a prosecutor might dig up the time you spent here, no matter how well you thought it was covered up." He glares at her parents with a disapproving glance that reminds me what a fucking badass Rafe is. Her mother fidgets in her seat.

"But he set her up. She wasn't dealing."

"It doesn't matter," Rafe adds. "She was arrested, and if they want to bring her back into this case, not only could her charges be dropped against him, but they could try to prove that she was involved with whoever is bypassing Hale's current shipments."

I know my place to stay quiet in the conversation because her parents would be quick to forget how I saved Sierra when they find out it was my supply she was paying back when she was arrested. She glances at me, and I can see her calculating.

"Hale would have good lawyers. What would happen if you offer him a plea for information on his supplier?"

"Sierra," her mother scolds her.

Rafe gives her a subtle smirk. He sees how bright she is. "We could clean up a lot of the drugs off Wickett for good."

"But what if he comes after her again? Who is going to protect her?"

Sierra looks at me. She has the same question in her eyes.

"I will," I say, feeling the words come from somewhere deeper.

She smiles.

"We can issue a restraining order, and in all honesty, Mr. and Mrs. Pearson, Hale will have to disappear from Wickett for good. Once he outs his suppliers, he will have much bigger fish to fry than a vengeance with Logan or Sierra."

"So, if I don't press charges, you can use the information you have for a better chance of keeping the drugs off Wickett for good," Sierra says proudly.

"I won't persuade you either way, Ms. Pearson."

I notice her parents getting uneasy behind her. This stuff makes them uncomfortable. They don't do police stations and face-to-face. They handle their legal business behind closed doors with a checkbook instead of a hearing.

"You have to make me a promise," Sierra says to Rafe.

He perks up his eyebrows as he waits for her demands.

"Do whatever you have to do to keep this town clean. I think he's been beat up enough to pay for what he's done, and I won't press charges. I just want to go home."

Her hand squeezes mine in her lap, like she can feel the way my heart drops when she says home. A reminder that Wickett is her vacation destination, not her permanent residence.

Chapter Twenty-Three

SIERRA

My parents are waiting in the car while I talk to Logan on the bench outside the station. They're waiting to take me home, to Newport, but my feet don't seem to want to move from the pavement.

Logan has shut himself off. I can feel it in the way he's avoiding my eyes. His jaw is clenched, and he has a tightness to his normally soft lips.

I touch his hand.

"Thank you," I mutter to get his attention. Just a couple hours ago, we were lip-locked and hungry for each other, but now...where do we stand?

"For what?" He glances up at me, and I can see the

pain behind his eyes.

"For saving my life, Logan. For changing my life. For... everything." I don't exactly want to be thanking him for deflowering me. It's not like it was a favor he did for me, but I feel desperate to bring up that moment for us. The first time we were together, the moment when we were both so lost and miserable that we buried ourselves in each other, finding more light and love there than we could have ever imagined.

And now, I'm not ready to let that go. If I asked to stay, would he want me? His harsh words about being a spring break fling were forced, I knew that, but what if there was some truth there?

"I think I should be thanking you," he answers, turning his body toward me so that he's hidden from my parents watching in the car. "I was at an all-time low when you arrived, Sierra. And if you hadn't forced me to snap out of it, then I don't know how much longer I would have had in the world."

"Don't say that," I whisper as I lean closer.

We feel like magnets, like the closer we get, the more the attraction pulls us together. Suddenly, my arms wrap around his waist, and I bury my face into his neck. His arms envelop me so that all I can smell is his cologne and the scent of him. I will never leave this spot, I tell myself.

There is a jingling of keys behind me. When I pull my face out of Logan's T-shirt, my cheeks wet with tears, I lock eyes with my dad who is standing there with a set of keys dangling from his fingers.

"What—" I ask.

"You've had a long day. Take the weekend to relax in the condo. Your mom and I will go back to Newport, but we expect you to answer any and all messages from us while you're here." He eyes Logan suspiciously.

My heart lurches in my chest. And I notice that my dad isn't handing the keys to me...he's handing them to Logan.

I turn toward him to gauge his response. "Thank you, sir," he replies. "But I have an apartment."

"I know you do," my dad answers firmly. "But this might be the closest thing you've had to a vacation, so take it." Logan looks at me, like he's asking me what he should do.

Logan is too proud to accept gifts or donations. He'll turn a million bucks away if he thinks he doesn't deserve it, but that's the problem. Logan doesn't think he deserves anything, and he deserves so much more than the keys to a weekend condo on the beach.

I put my hand to his back.

"Thanks, sir," he says to my dad.

My dad claps him on the shoulder. "Sierra doesn't do anything lightheartedly. She's not the kind of girl to waste her time on bad choices or whims. If she has put her faith in you...well..." My dad clears his throat. I've never heard him talk about me like that, especially while I'm standing right there. "It means you deserve it."

LOGAN

The apartment is bright, the windows floor-to-ceiling and overlooking the water. It's spotless and smells like delicate flowers and bleach, like the cleaning crew just came through.

I have no fucking clue what I'm doing here or why I accepted these keys. On one hand, this guy barely knows me, and I know his opinion of people like me. And yet, today changed the tides. We almost lost Sierra today, and as he handed me those keys, his eyes steady on mine, I could read the devastation there. It matched mine. The fear. The gratitude.

So, it wasn't about giving me a place to be alone with his daughter, it was about sending the message that he trusted me to be alone with her.

The sun is setting, leaving darkness hovering over the water, and in the dim light, I can see how tired Sierra is. She's been through too much today. Having a gun pointed at you, knowing your life could end too soon, is a sobering and terrifying experience that I would have never wanted for her.

We have a lot to talk about, her and I, but first, she needs rest.

"You need a bath and a bed," I say, pulling her into my arms.

"With you, right?" She smiles at me.

"Tonight, you rest. You've been through a lot today." I kiss her forehead.

Having her in my arms again feels rejuvenating, like

a fresh start, and maybe I can start afresh with Sierra. Maybe our worlds aren't too different, after all.

Even when I catch a glimpse of us in the bathroom mirror as I help her ready her bath. She's in a light athletic top and mint green yoga pants. My black leather jacket and dark brown hair looks all wrong in this bathroom, but I don't give a fuck anymore. Sierra and I may have come from different worlds, but we are creating an entirely new one together. One that lets her be the wild, little rebel she is and one that sets me free from the expectations that weigh me down.

I strip off my jacket just as she lifts onto her toes to kiss me. Her lips are soft, her kiss slow and hungry. My fingers trace the bottom of her shirt, pulling it up and over her head. A small squeak escapes her throat as she kisses me again.

Her hands are trying to undress me, but I hold her wrists in my hands. She gives me a devilish grin that I can't even think about right now.

"Bath. Bed," I say, though she's breaking my resolve.

"Join me," she pleads in return. I kiss her neck. I wouldn't trust myself to be naked in that bath with her, and I'd hate to make a big watery mess in the condo since it was so generously lent to us.

When she finally climbs in, deliciously naked, I hang my jacket from the door hook and sit on the side of the tub to take in her beautiful body submerged in the water. She keeps trying to lure me in like the little siren she is, but I manage to get her cleaned up.

My jeans are threatening to bust from the hard-on as

I lather her body, not missing even one curve. She lets out a moan when my soapy hands glide over the wet mounds of her breasts, and tries to guide my hand down to the warm core between her legs. Her head falls back with a sigh when I follow her lead, but then she gasps when I take my hand out of the water. Kissing her head, I reach for the towel.

"Baby, I'll do you one better."

Wrapping the towel around her wet body, I lift her hips around my waist as I carry her to the bed. Her lips are hot against mine, urging me on. She takes my bottom lip between her teeth, and I give her bare ass a quick smack. She whimpers, and I swear I'm not going to make it long.

When I drop her on the bed, I pull off my jeans and shirt, and she just watches like I'm putting on a show for her. Which is fine by me. My only goal is to give this girl as much pleasure as I can. I want her to stay in Wickett forever. I want to make her toes curl so much that she can't bear to even leave this bed. And soon enough, my bed.

I climb up onto the bed and hook my arms around her legs, lifting her pretty pink sex to my lips. She gasps when I lick the long folds from back to front, settling myself in on her clit.

As I tease her straight into a scream-worthy orgasm, I can't help but feel too damn lucky to have found this girl. On the outside, she seems so different, but it's the inside that matches mine. Her heart is my heart's equal.

Leaving her to recover from her first orgasm of the

night, I rifle through my jeans for the condom in my pocket. Once I have it wrapped and ready, I climb up to lay my body on hers.

She wraps her arms around my neck. "I want you inside me, Logan." The sound of my name in her ecstasy-laced voice nearly sends me over the edge.

I slide in smoothly. "Say it again," I mumble against the crook of her neck.

"Logan," she calls, throaty and full of need. "Logan, Logan, Logan."

Our bodies move together, finding rhythm and picking up a pace that throws us together into a shattering orgasm, and I link my fingers with hers.

I want to fuck away every terrible thing that happened to her today. I want her pleasure to erase all of the pain so that not an ounce of fear will be left, but as she intertwines her legs with mine, settling her head against my shoulder, I realize this girl never needs me to protect her. She doesn't need anyone to protect her. She won't be corrupted or shamed. Sierra won't break.

My girl is not that fucking delicate.

DELICATE

Epilogue

LOGAN

"I don't know how you put up with that relentless buzzing sound?" she asks, looking at me with those big blue doe eyes. I see it from my periphery, but I won't take my focus off of this tattoo—not for a second.

She hasn't flinched since I started. When the needle touched her skin, I saw her wince, and I wanted to stop, but she demanded I keep going, and what Sierra wants, Sierra gets.

After finishing the last bit of detail on the bird, a small swallow on the inside of her ankle, I place a kiss just above her knee.

"I hope you don't do that to all of your clients," she

whispers, her eyes gleaming at me.

"Only you, but this is it, young lady. We're not making this a habit." I cover her tiny tatt with A&D and cellophane and pull off my gloves. Then, I pull her long, beautiful legs around my waist and settle her onto my lap.

"It's adorable that you think I'm going to listen to you." She silences my argument by kissing me deeply as I wrap my arms around her waist.

"I love having you back," I say against her lips. I trail the kiss down to her neck, her collarbone, sliding my hands up her shirt and toward her breasts.

"I love being back, but don't get me started now. We don't have time. I have to open the shop in five minutes."

Naturally, I don't listen. Sex is the only time my strong-willed princess isn't so strong-willed. She doesn't put up much of a fight when I slide her panties to the side, and she even helps me unzip my pants. In minutes, I have her panting my name in my ear. I wish every work day could start like this.

"It's a good thing Murph is off today," she says afterward, fixing her skirt and putting her shirt back on correctly.

"Yeah, and I have a feeling with this new initiative the city council is dropping on us, he'll be out a lot. Which makes him very grumpy."

She throws her bag over her shoulder as she kisses me one more time before heading two doors down. I love having her just two doors away, but it makes working such a distraction. A lucky bastard like me doesn't just ignore the fact that the girl of his dreams is just a ten-second walk away. I can't help it when I sneak out of the shop and slide into the bookstore to get a taste of her lips.

Things don't normally happen so easily for me. My whole life has been one fight and failure after another. I fought for my brother and I failed. Until I just stopped fighting. When Sierra came along, I didn't deserve her, but that didn't stop her from pulling me from the lowest point I've ever fallen. Her love was my beacon and still is.

A couple hours later, Rafe and Murph show up at the shop together, which is surprising. We don't technically open for another couple hours, but I keep myself busy with commissions and sketches.

"You're coming with us," Rafe says with his arms crossed.

"You know it makes me nervous when you say that," I quip back with a smirk. "Where are we going?"

"It's kind of a surprise," Murph answers, which makes me laugh. Murph is not the kind of guy to do surprises.

It's a short car ride before we pull up to Murph's garage behind his big-ass house. This is when I start to get nervous—not because I think anything bad is in store, but because they've clearly done the math, and they know today marks my six months sober anniversary.

And it's Theo's birthday month.

They don't say a word as they get out of the car. I'm in

the passenger seat, and something is holding me back. Looking at these two guys who are standing by the garage door clearly talking about something, I feel the sudden inadequacy of my place in their group. I was the one to bring us back together, but I wonder if I'll ever feel like I truly fit in. I mean...I sold my bike for drug money, so I'm not really a fitting member of a motorcycle club.

But then again...Rafe is a cop.

And Murph is a mysterious millionaire.

So maybe we're just the strangest motorcycle club that's ever existed. But we did manage to nearly eradicate the sale of meth and heroin on the island, and that's not nothing.

"Get out of the car, kid!" Murph barks at me.

Quickly, I open the door and walk toward the two guys. They clap a hand on each of my shoulders. My eyes widen in anticipation.

"It's been a rough couple years," Rafe says.

"Let's not make a big speech out of it," Murph cuts in.

"I'm not, but we have to say something."

"Kid, you've earned this." Murph reaches into his pocket and pulls out his phone. A couple quick touches on the screen and the garage door starts to open.

I wait in anticipation, not daring to hope as I glance at the collection in Murph's garage. He has the truck and a collection of motorcycles in various stages of completion. I wonder briefly when Murph even has the time to build his bikes.

My eye catches on one bike that sits separately from

SARA CATE

the others. It's not his, but there's something familiar about it.

I gulp down the sudden emotion that lodges itself in my throat.

"He'd want you to have it," Rafe adds. "We just had to wait until you were ready."

My brother, tall and smiling, sitting on that bike, flashes through my mind, and I clear my throat to keep myself from completely falling apart.

"Go." Rafe pushes me toward the motorcycle.

As my hand slides across the worn leather, I let my eyes well up where the guys can't see. They'd be fucking crying too.

"I don't know what to say," I manage.

"You don't have to say shit," Murph says as he steps up next to me. "Just start her up and let's go for a ride."

"Fuck yeah," Rafe answers.

They fire up each of their bikes, and the three of us head out on a long ride around the island. And as fucking lame as it sounds, I can feel him there with us, on that ride.

SIERRA

I'm on the phone with the food vendor for our book fest event next month, when I hear the low rumble of a motorcycle park in front of the store. I sneak a glance at Mrs. Walker who is still dusting the new low shelves in the teen reading area at the back of the shop. She doesn't seem to even notice the deafening sound that now overwhelms our quiet store.

After I hang up, I check in with her to let her know that I'll be taking an early lunch.

When I step out front, I let a smile spread across my face as I take in the delicious sight of Logan leaning against a black motorcycle.

"Don't make me file a noise complaint," I tease him, my arms crossed.

"You're not surprised. Rafe already told you."

He says it like it's supposed to be a question, even though it's not. Of course Rafe told me. He had to brag about it to someone and it has been in the works for weeks. We worked together to keep Logan clean, but it was Logan who deserved the recognition.

With the support from his brothers and having me with him at the apartment, it's like Logan has the guts to be at his very happiest, and I'm loving every minute of it.

"Wanna go for a ride?" he asks.

"On that?" I smile.

I climb on the back, and he takes the same easy ride around the island as we did only six months ago.

When we reach the quiet beach on the suburban end, we walk down to the water where we shared our first kiss. He leans down and pulls me into a tight embrace, and I feel the gratitude in his touch.

"I love you," he whispers against my hair.

Taking his lips with mine, I try to taste those words,

what his kiss tastes like when he says them.

Since I moved back to Wickett six months ago, I haven't spent one day without kissing those words, and I never want to go another day without it.

"I love you too," I answer. Hand in hand, we walk back to where he parked the bike. I know we are still taking every day one at a time, and Logan will never be out of the dark when it comes to the addiction, but as long as I'm here, he'll have me to keep him afloat. And I plan to be here for as long as he is.

Bonus Epilogue

LOGAN

Three years later

My fucking hands won't stop shaking. What the hell is wrong with me? I've never been so goddamn hyped in my life, and I can't tell if it's nerves or excitement or downright terror. I keep waiting for her to take one look at me and realize this was a stupid choice.

"Breathe," Murph mutters from his place next to me.

I spot Rafe's shoulders shaking with a silent laugh.

I never should have picked these assholes. They're not helping at all. Nevermind that they're my best friends and I'd likely be dead without them, today I want to toss them both in the ocean.

They've both been through this already. I don't know what took me and Sierra so long. Our relationship started the fastest, a whirlwind week that changed our lives forever, but it's like we've been drawing everything else out since. Whatever the reason, my love for her has not wavered one bit since then. If anything, I've fallen even harder.

When I first met her I thought she was this delicate blonde rich girl, and I learned that under that soft and sweet exterior is the toughest, most passionate girl I've ever met. And she picked me.

There's movement on the pavilion, and the guests in their chairs stand in unison as the music starts playing, and I think I'm going to be sick.

Of course everything is picture perfect. She planned it that way. A small intimate ceremony on the beach with only our closest family and friends.

As I wait for her to make her appearance at the top of the aisle with her dad, I think back to the night I proposed. I wanted to make some grand gesture on my knee, maybe on Christmas morning, but the question just slipped out after an especially hot quickie when I came home from work late. I was still buried inside her when I pressed my lips to hers and asked her to be my wife.

She cried immediately, and I assumed I royally fucked up. I didn't have a ring. I didn't have a plan. I was such a typical screw-up that I couldn't even do the most basic of boyfriend duties.

But she shocked the shit out of me when she wrapped her arms around my neck and rang out, "Yes, yes, yes." I never wanted to pull out of her that night. I was too afraid if I let go of her for too long, she'd never come back.

Even now, as I wait to see her in that white dress, I'm scared as hell that she'll snap out of it.

Finally, she steps out of the pavilion and down the few steps to the beach where I'm waiting, and my whole world shifts on its axis. The most beautiful girl in the world with her sunshine eyes, sparkling smile, and stunning soul is walking toward me, looking straight at me, and I realize in that moment that somewhere in the past three years, she became a part of me.

Without her, I stop being Logan.

She brings out all the best parts of me, and I would gladly spend the rest of my life being the best version of myself for her.

I didn't even realize my eyes were misting up until she reaches to swipe the moisture from my cheek, and goddamnit it's hard as hell to not kiss her already.

I hardly register anything that happens after this moment. All I see is her eyes, and we are lost in each other's stare. She puts her hands in mine, and I look down to see my dark tattoos against her soft pale skin.

The minister talks a lot and Sierra squeezes my hand when I need to respond, and it's not until he says, "You may now kiss the bride," that I finally blink and pull Sierra into my arms and kiss her long and hard.

Our friends and family clap, and when I pull away, I

sneak a look at her parents who, given three years to get accustomed to me, are actually smiling. It's a far cry from the people who would have paid every penny in their bank accounts to get rid of me.

As Sierra and I walk hand-in-hand back up the aisle toward my bike waiting to carry us away, I feel the hard ring around my finger. "We're fucking married," I say with a laugh, and her face breaks out in a smile.

"I was afraid you blacked out during the whole ceremony."

"I think I did." We both laugh like we're high on this moment.

A moment later, we're on my bike. Her white dress is up around her thighs, and her veil blows behind us as we take off on our sunset cruise around the island. Our family surprised us with a honeymoon suite at the nicest resort in town. We'll have a beautiful view of the ocean from our bed, but I doubt I'll be looking out the window at all.

She tightens her arms around my waist as she rests her head against my back. I squeeze her hand.

Sierra is finally my wife, and I don't feel a bit different. I belonged to her the moment we met and she softened the hard, angry addict she met three years ago.

Once the sun goes down, we pull into the resort, and I carry her from the bike to our room, which is waiting with rose petals strewn across the floor and bed.

"Jesus," I mutter when I take it all in. She giggles in my arms, linking her arms around my neck.

As desperate as I am to lift this dress and fuck her as

my wife for the first time, I want to savor this feeling. The anticipation. So I take her to the window and drop her to the feet. There is still enough light in the sky to see the waves rolling on our private beach.

"This is beautiful," she whispers, and I pull her back against my chest. I grew up on Wicked, but I see the beauty in the beach so differently now, as if I'm seeing it all through her eyes.

For a moment, we stand there and watch the orange-and-blue-tinted waves roll in until I feel Sierra leaning back, rubbing her backside against me like she's accustomed to doing when she's feeling frisky, which is basically all the time. More often lately, which I figure is just due to her excitement with the wedding.

She turns her head back toward me, and I trail a kiss from her lips down her neck and shoulders. She hums softly. Her hand reaches behind her to stroke the growing stiffness in my pants. It doesn't take much. I'm almost always ready with her.

My fingers don't fiddle long with the zipper on her dress before it comes off easily, landing in a white heap on the floor.

I nearly lose it right there when I see that my girl is standing in front of me completely naked. I'm suddenly reminded of the first time she bared herself to me in my apartment in that ball gown with nothing on underneath.

"Sierra..." I scold, just like I did last time. "Where are your underwear?"

She bites her lip and looks up at me from under her

heavy lashes. "I didn't wear any."

"Tsk, tsk." Looking down at her, devouring that beautiful body with my eyes, I start unbuttoning my shirt, and she stares back like just watching me undress is enough for her. Leaning against the paned glass, she waits for me to undress, reaching for my belt buckle when I have my shirt off.

As soon as I'm stripped of my clothes, I reach for her, but she pulls away, grabbing the handle on the sliding glass door instead.

"This is a completely private beach, you know." Slowly, she pulls it open and a warm breeze hits me. I'm stark ass naked and standing at full attention. Walking outside is not exactly what I'm used to in this state.

"You can't be serious."

"We had our first kiss on the beach. Why not have our first married sex on the beach too."

"Are you sure no one can see us?"

She's already stepping out onto the sand before I can get an answer from her, but that's Sierra for you. Too bold for her own good and ten times braver than me. I watch from just outside the door as she runs toward the water. It's dark enough now that her moon-kissed skin is barely noticeable in the darkness.

"Husband of mine..." she calls, reaching a hand out for me. Obediently, I answer, walking across the sand to snatch her up and pull her naked body against mine. The cool water laps at my ankles as I lift her up and wrap her legs around me. Her kiss is hungry, and I feel her grinding her body against me.

Carefully, I lower her to the sand, and the first time the wave hits us, we both laugh. It's just enough of a shock to the system to add to the adrenaline. Teasing her with kisses across her body, she writhes beneath me when I finally reach the soft pink buds of her tits.

"Logan," she moans. "Please fuck me already."

"Yes, dear." I lift her leg under my arm and slide in easily, her pussy soaked with her arousal. We both cry out as our bodies become one. I love being inside her, and I wish it could last forever, but it never lasts long enough.

Resting my forehead against hers, I find my rhythm, moving deeper and harder with each thrust because I know that's how she likes it. It doesn't take long before her breathing becomes high-pitched, and I know she's close.

Like always, I pick up my speed and I lean back so I can watch her come undone. It's more beautiful than any sunset on any beach in the world. Her red-painted nails grip my biceps as she clings to my body and her legs tense around me. I couldn't stop from coming if I tried.

My heart stops, and when I pull back to look at her face, she's biting back a smile. I'm still inside her and she just made the world stop spinning.

Once upon a time that news would have terrified me. Made me feel guilty or angry, but right now, I feel like I've been given something I never truly felt before. A real family.

"Say something," she says as a tear slips out of her eye.

"I love you so much." I kiss her again, and this time I

don't miss it when my eyes start to fill with moisture too.

Sierra and I made this together. We got here with each other, and suddenly, I'm not questioning whether or not I deserve it or feel afraid she'll leave me. I fought my way out of a dark place, and I brought in all the light when I found her.

In the film reel of my life, she will be the star. From here on out and forever.

Barnes & Noble Booksellers #2791
235 Daniel Webster Hwy
Nashua, NH 03060
603-888-0533

STR:2791 REG:006 TRN:7225 CSHR:Parker G

BARNES & NOBLE MEMBER   EXP: 06/21/2023

Fear
  9780593125014   N
  (1 @ 10.99) Member Card 10% (1.10)
  (1 @ 9.89)   9.89
Addicted To You
  9781950165957   N
  (1 @ 14.99) Member Card 10% (1.50)
  (1 @ 13.49)   13.49
TOTAL   23.38
VISA   23.38
  Card#: XXXXXXXXXXXXX7387
  Expdate: XX/XX
  Auth: 025037
  Entry Method: Chip Card Tap

  Application Label: VISA DEBIT
  AID: a0000000031010
  TVR: 0000000000
  TSI: 0000

MEMBER SAVINGS   2.60

Connect with us on Social

Facebook- @BNNashua
Instagram- @bnnashua
Twitter-   @BNNashua

057.04B   05/29/2022 01:50PM

CUSTOMER COPY

warranty.

Returns or exchanges will not be permitted (i) after 30 days without receipt or (ii) for product not carried by Barnes Noble.com, (iii) for purchases made with a check less than days prior to the date of return.

Policy on receipt may appear in two sections.

Return Policy

With a sales receipt or Barnes & Noble.com packing slip a full refund in the original form of payment will be issued from any Barnes & Noble Booksellers store for returns of new and unread books, and unopened and undamaged music CD DVDs, vinyl records, electronics, toys/games and audio book made within 30 days of purchase from a Barnes & Nobl Booksellers store or Barnes & Noble.com with the belo exceptions:

Undamaged NOOKs purchased from any Barnes & Noble Bookselle store or from Barnes & Noble.com may be returned within 14 da when accompanied with a sales receipt or with a Barnes & Noble.co packing slip or may be exchanged within 30 days with a gift receipt.

A store credit for the purchase price will be issued (i) when a g receipt is presented within 60 days of purchase, (ii) for all textboo returns and exchanges, or (iii) when the original tender is PayPal.

Items purchased as part of a Buy One Get One or Buy Two, G Third Free offer are available for exchange only, unless all iter purchased as part of the offer are returned, in which case su items are available for a refund (in 30 days). Exchanges of the iter sold at no cost are available only for items of equal or lesser val than the original cost of such item.

Opened music CDs, DVDs, vinyl records, electronics, toys/game and audio books may not be returned, and can be exchang only for the same product and only if defective. NOO purchased from other retailers or sellers are returnable only the retailer or seller from which they were purchased pursua to such retailer's or seller's return policy. Magazine newspapers, eBooks, digital downloads, and used books a not returnable or exchangeable. Defective NOOKs may I exchanged at the store in accordance with the applicab warranty.

Returns or exchanges will not be permitted (i) after 30 days without receipt or (ii) for product not carried by Barnes Noble.com, (iii) for purchases made with a check less than days prior to the date of return.

Policy on receipt may appear in two sections.

DELICATE

Also by Sara Cate

Wicked Hearts Series
Delicate
Dangerous
Defiant

Age-gap romance
Beautiful Monster
Beautiful Sinner

Wilde Boys duet
Gravity
Freefall

Reverse Harem
Four

Cocky Hero Club
Handsome Devil

About the author

Sara Cate writes forbidden romance with lots of angst, a little age gap, and heaps of steam. Living in Arizona with her husband and kids, Sara spends most of her time reading, writing, or baking.

You can find more information about her at www.saracatebooks.com

CPSIA information can be obtained
at www.ICGtesting.com
Printed in the USA
BVHW041730100522
636644BV00001B/52

9 781956 830002